ON VESA

the airless moon, Jules and Yvette D'Alembert plan to
go their separate ways, investigating its diverse society

AT THE BOTTOM

Jules, under the alias Georges DuChamps, uses his
agility and strength to land a job at the spaceport. There
he is drawn into deadly conflict with the sullen, mysterious natives of Vesa's planet, Chandakha—only to make
a startling discovery.
Meanwhile . . .

AT THE TOP

Yvette, disguised as a wealthy widow, cruises on a
luxury starliner towards Vesa's underground pleasure
oasis, hoping to explore the vacationland that draws
millions of Empire tourists each year—and claims the
more unfortunate, forever! But Yvette is caught off
guard by an unexpected encounter, and suddenly finds
her life at stake . . .

AS AN UNKNOWN FORCE THREATENS
THE SAFETY OF EARTH'S EMPIRE,
THE D'ALEMBERTS
FACE THEIR MOST CHALLENGING
SPACE ADVENTURE!

NOVELS OF SCIENCE FICTION

by

E. E. "DOC" SMITH

•

The Lensman Series

CHILDREN OF THE LENS
FIRST LENSMAN
GALACTIC PATROL
GRAY LENSMAN
MASTERS OF THE VORTEX
SECOND STAGE LENSMAN
SPACEHOUNDS OF IPC
TRIPLANETARY

The Skylark Series

SKYLARK DUQUESNE
THE SKYLARK OF SPACE
SKYLARK OF VALERON
SKYLARK THREE

The Family D'Alembert Series
(with Stephen Goldin)

THE CLOCKWORK TRAITOR
GETAWAY WORLD
IMPERIAL STARS
STRANGLER'S MOON

STRANGLERS' MOON

E. E. "DOC" SMITH
with Stephen Goldin

A JOVE/HBJ BOOK

dedicated to my grandmother,
for spoiling me rotten!

S.G.

First Jove/HBJ edition published March 1979

Library of Congress Catalog Card Number: 76-15111

Printed in the United States of America

Jove/HBJ books are published by Jove Publications, Inc. (Har-
court Brace Jovanovich), 757 Third Avenue, New York, N.Y.
10017

CHAPTER 1

Predators and Prey

The Golden Crater Casino was unquestionably among the largest and plushest gaming palaces in the Galaxy. Its reputation for the exotic and the exciting was fully earned, as the briefest of walks down its crowded corridors and across its even more crowded rooms would reveal. People were jammed elbow-to-elbow in some places in their fanatical attempts to lose money to the House. Women in abbreviated costumes roamed the floor, ostensibly employed as photographers, waitresses and the like—though it was common knowledge that a fifty-ruble bill would procure other services from them as well.

The great and the near-great mingled at the tables, amid throngs of those who were merely wealthy but had aspirations toward greatness. Here a sensable star brushed against a countess; there a corporation president bumped into a famous news commentator. Rank and social distinction were of little importance in the casino; the only question of interest was how well could a person gamble and was luck on his side today?

Yet even as notorious and plush as it was, the Golden Crater was considered merely routine by comparison to other "establishments" on Vesa, the moon that billed itself as the "Playground to the Galaxy"—and which cynics called a variety of other names.

Nils Bjenden, a banker from the planet Lindstrom, stood to one side of a doorway looking with distaste across the crowded room. This chamber was so jammed with people that he had difficulty seeing the other side. The ceiling arched high above his head, and on it was projected a kaleidoscopic light show that continually changed colors with the changing noise level in the room. But he had not come here to look at the ceiling, he had come to gamble—and the mob on the floor was packed so densely that he could not see so much as a single gaming table.

"I told you we should have gotten here earlier," he said to his wife Karen, who stood beside him and looked as bewildered as he felt. Nils found he had to yell to be heard above the room's din, even though his wife was only centimeters away. "But you wanted to stop and eat first. We should have left when I wanted to."

"I didn't know it would be this crowded," she apologized.

A stranger who'd been standing behind them came to the woman's rescue. "Don't blame her, gospodin. The Golden Crater is like this around the clock. Vesa is 'the moon that never sleeps,' you know; these casinos are ample proof of that."

Nils grunted noncommittally and would have walked away, but Karen struck up a conversation with the man who'd saved her from a tongue-lashing. "You seem to know a lot about it. Do you live here on Vesa?"

The stranger laughed. He was a tall, thin man with brooding eyes and a dark complexion. His clothing was almost as conservative as Nils's, comprising a lightweight brown jacket and flared pants, a stiff white shirt and a gold sash tied about his waist. "No, gospozha, I don't think I'd care to. It's all too hectic, too busy; I'd go crazy in two weeks. I do travel a lot, though, and I come here fairly often—every couple of months, at least."

"This is our first time," Karen gushed. "I've been wanting to come for years and years—it's not as if we couldn't afford it. But Nils—my husband—is a banker, and he's always busy with one deal after another. You'd think the entire planet would fall apart without him there to look after it. I finally had to put my foot down and tell him that we were going to Vesa, now, or else."

"Hmpf," snorted her husband as he craned his neck to look over the throng of gamblers on the floor. "Some vacation it's been, too. I haven't had a moment to relax since we got here. There's always people, people, people. What did you say your name was, again?"

"Lessin," the stranger replied. "And if you think it's

6

crowded here you should see what it's like down on Chandakha."

It took a moment for Karen to realize what he was talking about. The moon Vesa was so famous that many people forgot there was a planet it circled. "Oh yes, I remember reading something about it on our trip out here. They've got an overpopulation problem, haven't they?"

"That's putting it mildly." Lessin closed his eyes and shuddered, as though recalling some personal nightmare. "Things are so bad down there that the people are little more than animals sometimes."

His tone made Karen shiver. "Then I'm just as glad I'm up here, among civilized people."

"I'm not," Nils grumbled. "I should never have left Lindstrom, not with that big deal about to go through. I don't like the thought of having to fight my way through that mob just to get near a table and do a little gambling."

"I quite agree," Lessin said amiably. "I much prefer the private clubs, myself. If I hadn't promised to meet a friend here, I'd be at one of them right now."

"I didn't know there were any private clubs," Karen said.

"Well, they certainly don't advertise—that's how they manage to stay private. They like to avoid crowd scenes like this one here."

"What are these private clubs like?" Nils asked.

"They're much smaller, more intimate places. Couple dozen people at most, and the atmosphere is more relaxed. The stakes can vary from moderate to high, depending on where you go, of course."

"Would there be any chance of our going to one of those places?" Nils asked. "There sure as hell isn't going to be any action for us around here."

The stranger hesitated. "Well, they *are* for members only. . . ."

"You're a member, aren't you?"

"Nils! You have no right to impose on this man," Karen complained.

"Oh, I don't mind. I was about to continue that the clubs are for members and their guests. I was going to be

7

taking my friend to one, but," he looked at his ring-watch, "he's more than half an hour late right now. If I know him, he's probably picked up one of the floorgirls and has forgotten all about me. I hate going places by myself. In fact, I had just about decided to invite you two nice people to come along with me."

"Yes, that's more the spirit," Nils said, rubbing his hands with gusto. It was obvious he preferred the thought of a quiet, dignified evening of gentlemanly gambling to the raucous atmosphere of the Golden Crater.

"It sounds lovely," Karen added.

"Fine, then it's all settled. Just give me a moment to get my cape from the checkroom and I'll be right back with you." Lessin smiled at them and moved off quickly toward one side of the chamber.

"We were lucky to meet him," Karen whispered to her husband. Her low voice was just barely audible above the noise of the casino. "He certainly seems to know what he's about."

"Very good sort," Nils agreed.

Their newfound friend was back three minutes later, a full-length brown fur cape draped elegantly over his tall, handsome frame. "Shall we be off?" he suggested.

As they left the casino and the door shut behind them, the drop in noise level was an immense relief. They faced one of the broad traffic corridors that carried the bulk of Vesa's public transportation. Being an airless satellite, all life on Vesa existed underground in the vast hollowed-out chambers and tunnels that honey-combed the moon. This tunnel was one of the major "arteries" and dozens of electric vehicles went past them each minute.

"Thank goodness," Karen said in the comparative quiet of the corridor. "I thought I'd burst an eardrum in there."

"It's not too long a ride to the club," Lessin said. "Let me see if I can flag down a jit." He stood on the curb and waved at a likely looking vehicle.

A large shuttle lumbered in their direction. This was one of the buses, or "jits," that were the universal method of transportation on Vesa. Jits were privately owned and operated, acting as combinations of cabs and busses; they could pick up passengers at will and take them anywhere on Vesa, without regard to fixed schedules. Tiny computers built into the driver's controls calculated the fare from the point of pickup to the destination.

This jit was obviously an old one, judging from all the paint peeling off its six-meter length. The glass in four of its windows had large cracks. As it pulled to a stop beside them, the group on the curb could see the vehicle's occupants—half a dozen seedy-looking men wearing dirty clothes. Most of them were in need of a shave. They leered out the windows at the well-dressed trio.

Lessin waved the jit away. "That's a problem you'd better be warned about if this is your first trip here," he explained. "Very few people have private cars; nearly everybody uses the jits because they allow for more flexibility in the traffic patterns. But there's a certain outlaw element that takes advantage of that. They'd think nothing of picking up newcomers like you, beating you up and robbing you. Hardly a week goes by without some story in the newsrolls about some tourist getting mugged on a pirate jit."

"Oh, dear," said Karen.

"I have heard about them," Nils said slowly. "That's why I carry a small stunner in my pocket at all times."

"A wise precaution," Lessin nodded. "However, sometimes a little prudence in one's choice of transportation can eliminate the need for that. Ah, there's a more likely candidate." He waved at another jit that was coming down the street.

This one proved to be much more acceptable to all of them. Not only was it new and clean, but the six passengers already aboard were far more respectable types who paid no notice to the new arrivals. Lessin insisted on paying the fares for all three of them as he gave the driver an address. "It'll only be a few minutes' drive," he told the Bjendens. "Just relax."

The couple from Lindstrom did so. There was little scenery to watch in these tunnels, but the shuttle's novelty intrigued them. Since it did not go faster than thirty

9

kilometers an hour—and since the climate was perfectly controlled within these corridors—the jit was an open-air conveyance with no roof. The slight breeze was deliciously cool as they drove along.

Two minutes later, the jit entered a solitary tunnel slightly darker than the main passageways. Lessin looked up and suddenly an expression of horror crossed his face. "Oh no!" he exclaimed.

"What's the problem?" Nils demanded.

"The ceiling's going to cave in! There's a crack in the roof right up there. See?" Both Nils and Karen craned their necks to see where the stranger was pointing.

At that precise moment, the other six men on the jit exploded into action. Two of them grabbed the Bjendens' feet, holding them tightly together so that they could not run. Two more grabbed their arms, pinning them to the sides to prevent struggling. The remaining two whipped yellow scarves off from around their necks and, in one lightning-fast gesture, twisted them around the throats of the married couple. The upward-tilted necks were well exposed—an easy target.

The two tourists were taken so much by surprise that they had no opportunity to struggle, even if the men holding their bodies had allowed such a thing. Their eyes bugged out of their sockets as the scarves tightened around their throats, squeezing shut the windpipes and cutting off their air supply. The only sound was the faintest guggling as Nils and Karen fought vainly to breathe.

The last sight either of them ever saw was Lessin's imperturbable face staring at them with neither pity nor regret in his eyes.

When both were quite dead, Lessin—as leader of the stranglers—had the duty of combing their bodies for loot. He did this efficiently and, within a minute, both bodies had yielded all that they had of value—wallets, jewelry and keys to a hotel room where more of their goods would be stored.

The shuttle driver's timing was impeccable—just as the leader finished his search, the jit pulled up to a large white building. Driving into a private accessway, the driver tooted his horn sharply twice, and a side door opened. Four men dressed in white coveralls emerged from the building and boarded the jit. They looked down at the two dead bodies and, without comment, lifted them up and carried them back outside. Lessin gave them a curt nod as they disappeared inside the building with their burdens and the door slid shut once more.

As the jit backed out into the main thoroughfare again, the leader of the strangler band sat down in a seat behind the driver. The Bjendens' hotel keys jingled idly in his hand. Tomorrow, after their rooms had been thoroughly picked over, the Bjendens would be "checked out" of their hotel and would simply vanish from the face of the Universe, as many thousands had done before them. Very simple, very routine.

Lessin gave an involuntary yawn. The banker and his wife brought his daily total to six. He decided to see whether he could bring that number up to eight before calling it quits. Stifling a second yawn, he told the driver to head back to the Golden Crater; the pickings there seemed exceptionally good today.

The man known as Garst was fuming silently as he strode down the marble-floored hallway. He made no effort to quiet the clacking sound of his boots made with each impatient step he took; he was angry, and he wanted his anger to show.

Her timing is lousy, he griped silently. *Just when I finally had a chance to talk with the emissary of the Countess von Sternberg. It would have been my big opportunity to break out of my dependence on one little moon, a chance to reach for bigger things.*

But maybe that was precisely why she had called him. Maybe she didn't want him branching out beyond her grasp. Marchioness Gindri was a very possessive person, and the thought that her own personal lackey might have ambitions to something higher than her would be a very deep sting. *But I'd tried so hard to keep this meeting secret.*

He stopped as he came to the giant doors that marked the entrance to her boudoir. These doors stood nearly three meters high, and were elaborately carved out of solid whitewood and gilded in ornate designs. The knobs were solid gold, sculpted in the shape of miniature birds flying with wings outstretched. The doors were meant to impress the visitor, but Garst had been here too many times before and they seemed just like doors to him.

He paused outside the portals to catch his breath and curb his temper. Maybe her summoning him now was just a coincidence. She'd called for him before at odd times, this could be just another one. She was, after all, none too bright; it would do him no good to allow his guilty conscience—or what passed for a conscience in him—to ascribe to her a cunning she did not possess. Probably the biddy was just suffering from another of her incessant loneliness jags and needed his services.

Garst shuddered. That was perhaps the most distasteful aspect of his entire operation—making love to her gross, overindulged body. Someday, he was afraid, his sensibilities would overcome his logical mind and leave him incapable of even performing the act.

He sighed. The truth of the matter was that he needed her to make his strangling operation work. The Marchioness controlled the entire moon, at least nominally. It was she who gave orders to the police force, the hotel employees and the casinos. True, he was the one telling her what orders to give, but without her authority and her title to back up those orders, he was lost.

Once again, the delightful thought of killing her flashed through his mind. Many were the times he had fantasized the simple act of reaching his hands out to surround her fat, multi-chinned neck and squeeze the life out of her. But, though the personal satisfaction that act would give him would be enormous, the consequences would be disastrous. Gindri had no direct heirs to inherit her title, and at her death Vesa would revert back to the Throne, allowing the Emperor to choose whomever he wished as the new Marquis. Knowing Stanley Ten's reputation for incorruptibility, the appointee would be someone Garst would never get a hold over.

He sighed again. His success lay in keeping Gindri alive and happy, so that she would not interfere with the profit-

12

able setup he had established. Garst was, if nothing else, a realist.

With his temper now well under restraint, Garst pulled down on the handles and opened the huge twin doors. Instantly the sickening stench of the Marchioness's perfume assailed his nostrils, and he had to fight down the impulse to gag. Instead, with his most obsequious smile plastered tightly onto his lips, he entered the room and snaked his way over to the side of the bed.

Marchioness Gindri Lohlatt of Vesa looked like nothing so much as a beached whale in a white satin nightgown. She easily massed a hundred and fifty kilograms; Garst had never asked exactly how much, more out of fear of being revolted by the actual number than out of politeness. Her fat face was always red and jowly, her many chins overlapping and virtually hiding her neck in layers of blubber. Her body was as soft and pallid as a slug's. She would hardly even be able to move on any world with a normal gravity, Garst thought. Only the fact that the gravity on Vesa was a mere one-quarter Earth standard allowed her to survive without a heart attack.

"You called for me, Your Excellency?" he asked as nicely as he could.

"Yes," she said. Her voice was a throaty rasp, escaping from deep inside her throat. She reached out one ponderous arm to him and extended a hand as round as a balloon. Garst brought the hand to his lips and kissed it.

He wanted to drop the hand after the kiss, but the Marchioness gripped his hand tightly with her own and pulled him closer to the side of her bed. The stench of her perfume grew ten times worse with each centimeter closer he came.

A silence hung in the air for a long moment, until Garst's impatience got the better of him. "May I ask, Your Excellency, why you sent for me at this particular hour? Though the urgency of matters of state of course pales beside my desire to please you, there are still some details that are important and must be done at certain times."

Marchioness Gindri looked up at him with great, rheumy eyes. "You haven't been to see me in three days."

13

Her voice wavered, as though she were on the verge of tears. "I need to know that you still love me."

Though his outward expression did not alter, Garst's inward fuming resumed at an increased level. *This stupid sow called me all the way over here for that?* he thought. *Oh, how good it will be when I can get away from this moon and start out in business on my own.*

"Of course I still love you," he said aloud, seating himself on the little bit of edge next to the woman's enormous body. "What is there not to love about you? You're beautiful, intelligent, personable, wealthy and powerful—everything I admire most in a woman." *And if you believe that, I deserve the Galaxy Award for acting.*

But the Marchioness saw no falseness in his words or eyes, and was reassured of his continuing affection. Spreading her arms apart to welcome him to her bosom, she said, "Come to me then, my lamb, and prove your love for me."

With thoughts darker than the blackness of space, Garst crawled into her arms. *I won't always be stuck on this miserable little rock—and when that day comes, I'll see that you get the rewards you've earned. Just wait.*

CHAPTER 2

The Problem with Vesa

As *La Comète Cuivré* drifted purposefully through the void of interplanetary space toward its rendezvous, its two occupants were keyed to the breaking point with eager anticipation. Yvette and Jules d'Alembert had been "on vacation" for three months—far longer than they would have liked—and they were itching for action.

"I wonder what we'll be up against this time," Yvette speculated aloud. "Are there any more grand dukes plotting against the Throne?"

"Probably nothing so dramatic," her brother smiled. He spoke in the French-English patois that was their native tongue. "After all, it doesn't take a direct threat against the Emperor's life to endanger the peace. There's always a long, uphill battle against entropy."

They stopped speaking as their radarscope indicated they were nearing their destination. Jules quickly computed the approach pattern and laid it into the ship's computer. The action was followed moments later by a flashing light on the control panel in front of them and, five seconds after that, a short blast from the retro-rockets. *La Comète,* according to the numbers flashed on Jules' screen, would be docking with the other ship in four minutes, thirty-seven seconds.

"Let's see what she's like out there," Yvette said, reaching for a different switch. Both turned their heads and watched a panel to the right of their seats as a vid-screen that had been dark suddenly jumped to life. Though they had known intellectually what to expect, they still could not stifle the gasps of awe as they gazed at the ship they were approaching.

The *Anna Liebling* was easily the biggest private space-going vessel they had ever seen. The d'Alemberts had grown up among circus ships that had to carry all the personnel and equipment of the Greatest Show in the Galaxy, monstrous fat freighters ranging up to a hundred meters long. That was considered the maximum size for any ship that had to maneuver through an atmosphere and land on the surface of a planet, and they had never thought they would behold anything bigger short of a battle cruiser. But now they did.

The ship before them looked like a giant rectangular box a hundred and twenty-five meters long and perhaps fifty wide and deep. Its outer hull was dull and pitted from uncounted billions of encounters with micrometeoroids. It was a ship that could only have been constructed in space, and would never be able to land. The dartlike sliver of the ten-meter-long *Comète* seemed terribly insignificant beside the space behemoth.

"Wow," Yvette whispered softly. "Rank certainly doth have its privileges."

As they came closer to the enormous vessel, part of the hull slid open and, like modern Jonahs, the two d'Alemberts and their ships were swallowed intact by the space-going whale.

The hull closed again behind them as their ship came to rest inside a giant hangar next to several other small shuttles that served to take the *Anna Liebling*'s passengers to and from the ship. From one of the hangar's walls a long metal tube three meters in diameter snaked toward the d'Alembert vessel and attached itself firmly to their airlock hatch. This shuttle room was simply too big to use as an airlock; it would require too much time and energy to pump air into and out of it each time it was used. So it was left free of air, and these transit tubes allowed passengers to walk to and from the shuttles without donning spacesuits.

"All right," Jules said as the tube wheezed its airtight connection onto their lock, "let's find out what the Head has in store for us."

Dressed as they both were in the routine gray spacer's coveralls that fit them only loosely, neither Jules nor Yvette d'Alembert looked like what they truly were—the two most capable, most highly trained secret agents in the Galaxy. Both were a trifle too short when compared to the standard Earther height these days—Jules stood at a hundred seventy-three centimeters while his sister was ten centimeters shorter—but that was because they weren't from Earth. Both were natives of DesPlaines, that harsh mining world with a surface gravity three times that of Earth normal. Over the course of the fourteen generations their family had lived on that planet, they had adapted well to life under extreme conditions.

Under their loose-fitting outfits, their bodies were packed with solid muscle, tested to withstand the grueling pull of their world's gravity. Their reflexes were lightning fast, as they had to be—on a planet where objects fell at such an increased rate, even a slight stumble could be fatal. The d'Alemberts' bones were thicker and harder than an Earth person's, their sinews tougher, their muscles stronger.

But there was more to their heritage than just tough bodies. For the d'Alembert family had, for the past two centuries, operated and starred in the Circus of the

Galaxy, the number one attraction throughout human-occupied space. Jules and Yvette had been the premier aerialists for the Circus for over a dozen years, their already perfect bodies honed to clinical precision by the intensive training and impossible demands of their art.

Several months ago, though, Jules and Yvette had left the Circus. There was no outward sign that they had departed, for their younger cousins had stepped in to become the new "Jules and Yvette," while the old ones—as their predecessors had before them—moved up to their real jobs: undercover agents for the Service of the Empire.

Almost from its inception, the Circus had provided SOTE with its top agents. The specialized skills its performers possessed were ideal for the jobs that the Service needed done. Added to that was the fact that the d'Alembert family, led by Duke Etienne d'Alembert, had always been extremely intelligent and unquestioningly loyal to the Throne, and that the Circus was able to travel all over the Galaxy without arousing suspicion. The Circus was SOTE's secret weapon against the forces of disorder, with the emphasis on the word *secret*. Only a handful of people knew about it—and since that handful comprised the Imperial family, the Head of the Service and his chief assistant, that secret was well-kept indeed.

As Jules and Yvette emerged from the transit tube they found the chief assistant waiting for them. Duchess Helena von Wilmenhorst was obviously bred of Earth—tall, willowy and beautiful, with her long black hair tied into braids behind her so that it wouldn't be in her way on the ship. Apparently not all portions of the *Anna Liebling* were under ultragrav as this part was.

Helena strode quickly toward them. Her brown- and peach-colored pants suit emphasized the beauty of her body quite nicely, Jules noticed with a smile. She came straight over to him, put her slender arms about his waist and gave him a warm hello kiss. "It's good to see you again," she said in Empirese, the Russian-English mixture that was the Galaxy's official language. "How's your leg, Jules?"

Jules reached down and patted his left calf. "Almost as

17

good as new. Those regeneratives the doctors have now are incredible. They tell me that in another month or two I'll never even know I was blaster-burned." He and his sister spoke Empirese as flawlessly as DesPlainian.

"Glad to hear it. You fought too gallantly there to deserve a permanently gimpy leg." Helena turned her attentions to Yvette, embracing her as well and exchanging pecks on the cheek. "And how are you, my darling Evie?"

"Fine physically, but impatient I'm afraid. Vacations are smooth for a while, but they can get boring too quickly if there's no work in between. I'm dying for some action."

"You'll get it," Helena promised. "There's no shortage of work for any of us. Father just wanted to make sure you were all recovered from that last bout before sending you out again. You'd better follow me now; he's waiting for us."

Helena led the way down the maze of corridors that honeycombed the ship. Jules and Yvette were astounded at just how luxurious a space yacht this size could be. Paintings by some of the Galaxy's most famous artists were set in niches along the hallways. One long corridor wall, extending more than fifteen meters, was a single mural depicting a breathtaking sunset across a plain on some alien world. Holobiles, those three-dimensional color laser images, hung from the ceiling, their abstract shapes revolving in an imaginary wind. The air smelled faintly of jasmine, though the scent was subtly different.

But the surprising thing was that they encountered no other people along their path. The corridors had the feel of well-traveled routes, yet not a soul was anywhere to be seen. Their three pairs of footsteps echoed hollowly against the metal walls that lined the passages.

When Jules remarked on their solitude, their guide nodded and summed up the situation in one word: "Security. The *Anna* has a crew of over three hundred, but we had these corridors sealed off for you. Remember, you're our secret weapons; even though everyone aboard is trustworthy plus, we don't want your faces

18

even associated with SOTE if we can avoid it. The fewer people who know your connection, the safer you'll be.

"Here we are now," she continued, leading the d'Alemberts up to a plain metal door labeled simply "Room 10." "This is where everything comes together. Father thought we could talk here in the most secrecy."

As the door slid open, it revealed to the two agents a room that awed them with both its size and its functional beauty. Cylindrical in shape, the chamber had a diameter of fifteen meters and extended upwards for ten. Along the walls a spiral rampway led from the floor to the ceiling, with banks of computer terminals and readout screens spaced closely together along the ramp. Doors at various levels led out to other parts of this immense spaceship, for this was obviously the nexus of all activity aboard.

Seated at a small console in the center of the floor, looking dwarfed by the empty vastness of this nerve center, sat Grand Duke Zander von Wilmenhorst, the Head of the Service of the Empire. The conservative navy blue body-tunic he wore seemed to make him even more anachronistic in this overwhelming room of flashing lights and rampant technology. His basic humanity was out of place amid these machines.

Physically he was rather ordinary in appearance, being of medium height and build, but his almost totally bald head gleamed in the bright lights. It was his eyes, though, that were his most outstanding feature, for they could not disguise, even to the most casual observer, the overwhelming intelligence that lay within that skull. Zander von Wilmenhorst was the master tactician of the Galaxy—which was why he headed the Emperor's most select group of agents.

But at this moment the Head chose to be neither a grand duke nor a boss; he greeted Jules and Yvette almost as his own nephew and niece. "It's good to see you both again, and looking so healthy," he said after gallantly kissing Yvette's hand and shaking Jules' firmly. "I apologize for the sumptuous surroundings; I prefer doing business in my office, but this was the most secure spot on the

19

ship and the two of you merit the best. I sometimes get to play admiral here."

Yvette looked around and could indeed visualize the room as it might look during a crisis situation: hundreds of men and women bustling to and from their battle stations, the low buzz of continental conversation, the clacking of feet upon the metal flooring, the quiet chaos of a communications center. And in the very middle of it all, supervising every minute detail would be the Head himself, eyes gleaming as he snapped out each quick order.

She blinked and the scene vanished. There were just the four of them here—four friends in casual conversation. The Head guided them over to some chairs and they sat down, Yvette and Jules in front of the console and Helena behind and a little to the left of her father.

"I suppose you realize that I didn't call you here just for a social visit," the Head began. "Much as I like your company, the Galaxy forces us to work. Have you ever heard of Vesa?"

"Who hasn't?" Jules replied. "It's one of *the* top resorts in the Galaxy, the playground of the super-rich. It's a pretty wild place, from what I hear. Wide open; you can do almost anything there if you've got enough money or influence."

"The Circus has never played there, though," Yvette added. "At least, not during our lifetimes. As soon as Vesa started getting a reputation it decided it could do without such 'simple' entertainment as ours. We're not sophisticated enough for them, so they don't ask us to come."

The Head nodded. "Yes, and that complicates my job a little. Ordinarily I'd send the Circus in there so that your whole family could find out what the problem is. But as things stand, it'll have to be just the two of you. Do you feel up to it?"

"Do stars shine?" Yvette said. "We've been getting impatient for weeks. I feel ready to lick ten Banions single-handed."

"Hopefully that won't be necessary. Banion the Bastard spent years developing that traitors' nest you smashed,

20

covering most of the Galaxy. This is just a localized problem that I want to keep from getting out of hand."

The Head drummed his fingers on the top of the console for a moment and looked at them, wondering where to begin. Finally he continued on, "As you're well aware, the Service is not a police agency. Our primary concern is the safety of the Empire and the Emperor, not the enforcement of local laws. The Stanley Doctrine laid down by Stanley Three clearly—and wisely, in my opinion—delegates the responsibility for law enforcement to the local nobility, as representatives of the Emperor. We manage to hold the Empire together by the simple expedient of not getting involved in local matters. 'That Emperor is best loved who stays away from his people's business,' to quote Milney.

"On the other hand, we can't close our eyes to everything. The Empire runs on interstellar commerce. When the relationships between worlds are affected, it *becomes* the Emperor's business—and consequently the Service's as well. And that, I'm afraid, is where Vesa comes in."

The Head stood up and paced around behind his desk. "The planet Lindstrom has recently been negotiating a big agricultural deal with Appeny, one that would involve trillions of rubles on both sides. I won't bore you with the details, they're quite extensive and beside the point. The matter was being negotiated largely through the auspices of one man, Nils Bjenden—Lindstrom's most influential banker. It was to be his bank that would guarantee the financial outcome; but more than that, it was his personal integrity that was keeping both sides interested.

"Three weeks ago, Nils Bjenden and his wife disappeared. The deal between the two planets fell through, causing severe economic hardship to both worlds. I emphasize that no one stood to gain by their disappearance; it caused a disaster all around. This is the point where the Service got interested. After all, a fiasco of this size will have economic repercussions throughout the rest of the Galaxy as well, and we don't like that. So the chief of the Service on Lindstrom began investigating to find out why the deal had failed and what had happened to the Bjendens."

The Head stopped his pacing and moved in front of the console. Planting his feet firmly in front of the table, he leaned back against it, looking directly at the d'Alemberts. "It turns out," he said, "that the Bjendens decided to take a short vacation just before closing the deal. Being very wealthy, they decided to go off-planet and, never having been there before, they decided to visit Vesa. They left a clear trail that far; any number of people saw them on the spaceliner to Vesa, and there is a record of their having checked into a hotel there. But from that point on, nothing is clear. Suddenly there is no further record of them at their hotel, or at any other. Their return trip tickets were cashed in, and there is no record of them buying new ones. All of a sudden, Vesa just swallowed them up, without a trace. That was all our man on Lindstrom could determine from where he was, so he referred the case—with a Class Four Priority—to the SOTE branch on Chandakha."

"Chandakha?" Jules interrupted. "Where's that? I thought I'd heard of most of the planets, but that sounds like a new one."

"It's interesting how these things work out," the Head said, smiling at Jules' confusion. "Everybody knows that Vesa is a moon, but it's become so famous that it has figuratively eclipsed the planet it circles. Chandakha is a planet slightly larger than Earth itself. It was settled some three hundred years ago mostly by people of Asian stock —particularly those from the Indian subcontinent. Chandakha has always been a relatively poor world; the people can raise enough food to feed themselves, but they've had little commerce with the rest of the Galaxy. Vesa is their big drawing card, and it gets all the attention.

"At any rate, our SOTE chief on Chandakha, Marask Kantana by name, received the report from Lindstrom and, since it had a high priority, she got right to work on it. Because Chandakha has always been such a quiet world she had a very small staff, but she did what she could. She checked all the standard places, and came up with the same answers as the Lindstrom chief—namely

22

that the Bjendens had simply vanished. The local Vesan police more or less shrugged their shoulders and told her there was nothing they could do—with so many transients coming and going all the time, it was impossible for them to account for any particular ones. They were very polite, but their total lack of cooperation infuriated Kantana and, shrewd woman that she is, she decided to look into matters a little further.

"What she found simply astonished her. She double-checked, cross-checked, practically wove herself into a plaid with all her checking. When she was positive her facts were irrefutable, she sent them back here to Earth —this time with a Class Eight Priority."

Jules and Yvette cast each other startled glances. A Class Eight Priority was nothing short of a planet-wide catastrophe. Suddenly this case had taken on much more dire dimensions than just the disappearance of a banker and his wife.

Reaching down onto the surface of the console, the Head picked up three bookreels. "These are her findings," he said. "They came straight to Helena on arrival, and she brought them instantly to my attention. I'll give them to you before you leave; they'll probably shock you as much as they did us. There are a few more reels, also, because we correlated some data of our own. The total picture is frightening."

He went back and sat down behind the console, never taking his eyes from the d'Alemberts' faces. "The disappearance of the Bjendens was no isolated phenomenon. Over the past twenty years more than two hundred and fifty thousand people have vanished on Vesa without a trace!"

Jules sat bolt upright and Yvette's eyes widened in disbelief. "What?" the female agent exclaimed. "That's impossible!"

"I don't believe it," Jules said, echoing his sister's sentiments. "That many people can't simply disappear."

"Nobody said it was 'simple'," Helena spoke up from behind her father. "In fact, we suspect it's awfully complex—a full-fledged conspiracy."

"There's no other explanation," the Head agreed. "It's

23

so unexpected that no one ever looked for it before. But a simple check of spaceliner reservations tells a good deal of the story. Over the last two decades a certain number of tourists have come to Vesa and a certain number have left. The first number is quite larger than the second."

"Maybe they stayed on Vesa," Yvette suggested.

"Unfortunately the answer is not that simple," said the master tactician, shaking his head. "The population of that moon is well accounted for. We have records on births, deaths, immigrations and emigrations for that entire timespan, and they entirely explain the present population level."

"But why wasn't this noticed earlier?" Jules asked. "Didn't the spaceship companies think anything was odd when so many people canceled their return reservations?"

"Apparently not. The customer is always right, and it's not polite to pry into his reasons for canceling. Perhaps he's decided to stay longer, perhaps he's decided to book passage with another company. Remember, this was happening gradually, and the effect was spread out over all sixty-two companies that run ships to Vesa. They just never compared notes among themselves. It wasn't until we compared all their records together that we noticed the discrepancy."

Yvette found herself shaking her head. "But how can such a huge number of people just disappear without an alarm being raised? Some of them *must* have had family and friends who would miss them. Why weren't the police notified?"

"Ah, but they were. Our Central Computer Facility has the records of every police department on every planet, and we cross-checked their missing persons files. They're simply bulging with cases of people who went off to visit Vesa and never returned home."

"But if that's the case. . . ." Jules began.

"I know; it looks like incompetence on someone's part not to have spotted the pattern long ago. But really, what reason was there to cross-check before? Look at it this way: there are at present one thousand, three hundred and forty-three planets in the Empire. If we assume randomness, that equal numbers of people from each planet disappeared on Vesa, that leaves us with an average of two hundred people per planet. Now average that over twenty years, and you find that only ten people per planet per year are disappearing there. Not an extraordinary number at all. The ordinary planetary police force handles thousands of missing person calls in a year. I assume that, when they trace a missing person to Vesa, they put in a routine call to the police there for assistance. The Vesan police give them the same polite brushoff they gave Kantana. The planetary police have neither the time nor the resources to follow up on these cases, so they mark them unsolved and stick them away. Ten unsolved cases per year is a drop in the bucket compared to the volume they're used to handling."

Yvette and Jules sat in stunned silence as they contemplated what the Head had told them. A quarter of a million people had gone to Vesa and vanished. Furthermore, they were disappearing at a rate of better than twelve thousand a year—or thirty-five a day! What could be happening to them all?

"You're implying," Jules said slowly, "that the Vesan police are in on whatever conspiracy is occurring there."

The Head folded his hands on the table in front of him. "There's simply not enough information to say. It's extremely likely that they know something. After all, no matter how many tourists they say they get—and I will concede it's an awfully large number—it's hard to imagine them not noticing something of this magnitude. But it's rather obvious that they're choosing to ignore it."

"And if they're doing that," Yvette mused aloud, "then they must be taking orders from someone. The most likely suspect is the person in charge. Let's see, Vesa is a moon, so it would have to be a marquis—correct?"

"A marchioness, in this case," the Head nodded. "Marchioness Gindri Lohlatt, a spineless sort at best. Our personality profile shows her to be incapable of any sustained conspiracy like this; she's simply too weak-willed. She may be someone else's tool, but it's doubtful she's the brains."

"A duke, then," Yvette persisted. "The Duke of Chandakha, perhaps?"

"The Duke of Chandakha is thirteen years old," the Head informed her. "His mother has served as Regent since he assumed the title two years ago. The former Duke was assassinated by a disgruntled peasant after a reign of thirty-four undistinguished years."

"In other words," Jules said, "since this activity on Vesa has continued unabated for twenty years, it's probably unconnected to the Dukes of Chandakha."

The Head nodded. "There's a basic lack of continuity in the two regimes, yet the records indicate that the disappearances didn't even slow down at the Duke's death."

"Then the answer is definitely on Vesa." Yvette's words were more a statement than a question.

"Yes. Since the resorts on Vesa account for well over ninety percent of Chandakha's wealth, the Dukes of Chandakha have always been subservient to the marquisate of Vesa. They need the tax revenues too badly for their own survival."

"At the risk of stating the obvious then," Yvette said, "I gather our assignment is to find out what's happening to all these missing persons and put a stop to the operation."

"Exactly." The Head set his jaw, and fire gleamed in his eyes. "The thought that this vast a conspiracy could be going on right under our noses for so long without our even being aware of it is galling. At least with Banion we knew he existed, even if we couldn't track him down. But this—" he spread his hands "—this is like them painting over our eyes and daring us to do something. I don't like being blinded while somebody makes a fool of me." The Head stood up, determination written in every line of his face.

"That's why I want you, my two best agents, to handle the case. I want this menace smashed, and I want it done quickly!"

Back in their own ship again and floating free in orbit around Mother Earth, the two d'Alemberts studied the reels their boss had given them. Document after document reiterated what they had already been told—that somehow, thousands of people were simply ceasing to exist.

The supersiblings had found from long experience that talking the case out aloud between them helped clarify their thoughts. "Let's look at a typical case," Jules was saying. "Say Ivan and Tatyana Gregorov go to Vesa. Their spaceship reservations are all paid for, round trip. They check into their hotel and spend a few days gambling and seeing some of the shows. Then, before their vacation is supposed to be over, they abruptly check out of their hotel, taking all their belongings with them. They cancel their return reservations, getting cash for the tickets. And that's it, they're never heard from again."

"Where are they all going?" Yvette mused. "Something must happen to them. They're not staying on Vesa, unless there's a secret underground city we don't know about. Maybe they're all being taken into slavery in the deep, dark pits of some treasure mine."

"Vesa's got all the treasure mines it needs right at its gambling tables," her brother pointed out. "More money changes hands here than on the Galactic Stock Exchange. Your imagination is running a little overtime, sis."

"But if the people aren't staying on Vesa, then they must be leaving—and the outgoing logs of all the ships departing from there indicate no such thing."

"Which leaves us in an impossible situation. The people aren't staying and they aren't leaving. They're simply vanishing."

"They could be dead, I suppose."

"Yes, it's a lot easier to hide a dead body than a live one. But even so, where do you stash a quarter of a million corpses so that they won't be noticed?"

"They must have some system to it. Vesa's an airless moon; maybe they bury them all in some crater on the surface where no one ever goes. Maybe they have a catapult that launches the bodies directly into their sun."

"You're beginning to sound desperate."

"Sorry; having brain cells chasing themselves around in circles inside my skull tends to make me dizzy."

27

"We're talking about thirty-five bodies a day," Jules said. "Disposing of them in any way like that would be a major industry, and terribly wasteful of energy. There has to be a simpler, more efficient method of going about it. But I'm damned if I can think of what it could be."

"Let's put that problem aside for the moment, before our brains turn to pink jelly. The one thing we know about this operation is that it's systematized. Anything with that rapid a turnover of business has to be. And wherever there's a system, there's a way to crack it; Papa's told us that often enough. We begin looking for common links. Is there anything the victims have in common?"

"Not a thing," Jules said shaking his head. "The victims are totally random. They come from all over the Galaxy. They're men, women, old, young, famous, obscure, all races, all religions. They have nothing whatsoever in common."

"One thing," Yvette said thoughtfully. "They all came to Vesa from somewhere else."

Jules floated in the middle of the cabin, staring at his sister in open-mouthed amazement. "Evie, you have the rare gift of spotting the obvious. Of course, they all had to be rich. Only the super-affluent can afford to go someplace like Vesa. And that means. . . ."

"That money has something to do with it," Yvette said, completing her brother's thought. "These people are being killed and robbed of whatever they brought with them, then disposed of somehow."

"Yes!" Jules exclaimed, but then his expression changed. "No, wait a minute. That doesn't make sense. Vesa has no need to rob and murder people. The casinos gross so much money that they don't know what to do with it all—not to mention all the hotels, bars, theaters and brothels that have their own rakeoff. What's the percentage in killing people for their money when they're determined to give it to you legally?"

"How many casinos, hotels, bars, theaters and brothels are there on Vesa, *mon frère?* Two hundred? Three hundred? Four? Maybe even a thousand. What's the permanent resident population of Vesa? Fifty-some thousand, according to the most recent tape I saw. The legitimate operations probably earn a bundle for the minority of the people who own them and the larger majority who work for them. That still leaves an awful lot of the people wanting a slice of that pie. And it's such a rich pie that none of the fatcats minds them taking a small share. After all, there are about seven hundred tourists arriving on Vesa every day; who will miss a small fraction?"

"*Tu as raison,* as always. The percentage murdered is nowhere near high enough to adversely affect the take in the casinos, so they won't complain. The police are obviously getting paid off to remain stupid. The murderers get fat off their booty. Everybody wins, nobody loses— except, of course, for the poor victims who wander into the trap."

Yvette smiled weakly. "I'm not feeling nearly so dizzy anymore. It's good to know that this whole mess can be thought out logically."

"But just knowing what they're doing is a long way from smashing it," Jules said. "We still need to know how and who."

"A two-fold problem," Yvette nodded. "It seems tailor-made for a two-pronged attack. The 'how' appeals to me, I think. I could travel to Vesa in style, set myself up as a victim and see what I catch with my bait."

"That leaves me the 'who.' It has to be done by the ordinary people living on Vesa, that much seems obvious. I'll have to get a job there, join their ranks and see what I can learn. But what sort of job should it be?"

"Well, what are your qualifications? You're strong, athletic, agile, not too quick-witted . . ."

"I beg your pardon!"

". . . and obviously suited to manual labor," Yvette finished with a smile. "Not very well educated, but eager to make a lot of money without having to work hard at it. Just the sort of man who would turn into a thief and a murderer."

"With sisters like you," Jules muttered good-naturedly under his breath, "who needs enemies?"

29

CHAPTER 3

Locker Room Brawl

Spaceports on airless worlds all look pretty much the same. Such worlds are invariably pitted with craters from meteoroid impacts, and one of these craters is widened out and deepened to accommodate the landing of ships. Long airtight boarding tubes, similar to the one in the *Anna Liebling*'s hangar, allow the passengers to disembark down a sloping ramp to the interior of the spaceport without having to go through the inconvenience of donning cumbersome spacesuits.

The loading and unloading of cargo, however, is a much different matter, since freight will rarely walk down a ramp of its own accord. The procedure here is to have all cargo packed in airtight modular sections, usually stored in the lower portion of the ship. Upon landing, a large section of the ship's hull slides open, exposing the cargo to the vacuum of the planet's surface. Special cargo tractors emerge from the walls of the crater—enormous flatbed carriers equipped with their own cranes, winches and other apparatus. When the tractors reach the ship they disgorge dozens of spacesuited figures who begin transferring the cargo modules from the hold to the carriers, which then drive back to their hangars and unload the freight into airlock chambers. From this point, distribution of the materials can proceed normally. The entire operation is reversed, of course, for loading cargo onto an outbound spaceship.

The men who work the spacedocks are a breed apart. Strong, tough and hardworking, they nevertheless are quick and agile. They have to be—working in a spacesuit is awkward at best, hazardous at worst. They are usually a close-knit group, out of a sense for survival; working in a vacuum makes you very dependent on your comrades. Even the most trivial accidents can be fatal in an airless environment.

When Jules d'Alembert—working now under the name Georges duChamps—arrived on Vesa, one of the first places he applied for a job was the Vesa Spaceport. His references—all faked, of course—were impeccable, and impressed the personnel manager. Two days later, Georges duChamps received a call at the cheap hotel room where he was staying, telling him to report for work at 1730 the next day.

There were the usual preliminary forms to be filled out, and Jules was measured for a spacesuit. Fortunately, another DesPlainian had worked here several years before, and there was already a suit in stock that would accommodate the slight but important peculiarities of the DesPlainian body form. Once those tedious necessities were taken care of, the personnel secretary led Jules down a corridor to the office of his new boss.

The gang foreman was a hulking bear of a man named Laz Fizcono. He stood over two meters tall and massed a hundred and ten kilos, with a body that had never shirked a day of work in its life. His leonine mane of red hair topped a round, full face with bushy red eyebrows and a mangy beard. His eyes glittered with life as he looked Jules over appraisingly.

"Well, what have we here?" his voice boomed out as the personnel secretary brought Jules into his office. "A dwarf?" He extended a meaty hand in the direction of his new helper.

Jules calmly stood his ground as the bigger man approached. He correctly read the insult as a good-natured challenge to determine his personality. As foreman, Fizcono wanted to find out quickly just what sort of man this new fellow was, whether he had a quick temper, whether he would blow under pressure. A good boss knew the capabilities of all the people under him.

So instead of reacting to the epithet, Jules just smiled. "DesPlaines is a planet of big, blustery mountains," he said evenly. "We mine them anyhow. It'll take more than a giant to make me feel small."

He took the foreman's proffered hand firmly in his own. Fizcono squeezed it with all the massive strength his bear-like paw could muster. Jules accepted it without a wince

31

and, when the foreman had finished with his best shot, Jules began squeezing back. Fizcono's eyebrows lifted in surprise as the smaller man's strength was more than a match for his own. Jules just continued to stare up at the man a full thirty centimeters above him and smiled nonchalantly.

Then Fizcono did something unexpected—he laughed, a giant bellow that shook the walls of the tiny office. "By Fross, I like you, little man," he said. "You don't give in a millimeter, do you? Yes, he'll do nicely," he added to the personnel secretary, who left Jules' forms on the desk, smiled and returned to her own office.

Jules found himself liking Fizcono as well. The big man had an unforced affability that would make him a good and loyal companion. He would be a stern boss, but there was not a malicious bone in his body.

"Come on," said the foreman, leading Jules out of the office. "It's almost time for the shift to begin, and you'll want to meet the rest of your mates."

They moved down a maze of corridors, which Fizcono assured Jules he'd learn in a day or two, and eventually arrived at the suit-up room. There were ten men there already, and within the next few minutes twelve more arrived. Without exception the men were taller than Jules, and he took some good-natured ribbing from all of them when Fizcono introduced him as "my trained midget." But Fizcono's respect for him was also apparent, and the men took their cue from that. If the boss respected him, he must be good.

In general the men seemed to be from planets all over the Galaxy—a fact which was not too surprising, since Vesa was such a cosmopolitan center. It was a magnet drawing people from all over. But Jules very quickly noticed that one group of seven men kept very much to themselves. Their complexions were swarthy, their eyes darker and more brooding. There was a suspicion lurking in them against their coworkers, perhaps a smoldering resentment. The emotion was hard for Jules to read, but it was obvious that *something* was there.

One of the other men, a clean-shaven fellow named

Rask, noticed Jules eyeing the separatist group. "Haven't you ever seen Chandies before?" he asked.

"What are Chandies?" Jules didn't like the man's smug, superior tones. They gave evidence that all was not smooth within this work crew.

A third man joined them. It was obvious from his breezy familiarity that he was a crony of Rask's. Jules searched his memory and recalled that the man's name was Brownsend. "Chandakhari," explained the newcomer. "They're from that hick planet we're circling. Farmers, peasants. They stick together because they're afraid of real men."

The group of Chandakhari, having already suited up except for their helmets, walked past without a word, even though Brownsend's voice had been loud enough to carry to them. Jules was not sure how he should respond to this bigotry, but he was saved from having to by Fizcono, who came over as soon as he heard what was going on. "That's enough from you, both of you," the foreman said, glaring at Rask and Brownsend. "You'll work together or you won't work for me, it's that simple. I've told you that before. I hope," he added to Jules, "you won't pick up any bad habits from these two. They're good workers, but opinionated."

"I'm quite capable of forming my own opinions, sir," Jules replied. "I don't have to borrow anyone else's."

Fizcono gave an ursine grunt of satisfaction and moved on.

Despite the fact that Jules was in peak physical condition, he found the work that first day out on the sunfried surface of Vesa grueling. He was quite familiar with the loading and unloading of ships; after all, the Circus was constantly on the move, visiting a new world on the average of once every three weeks. When the circus gear was being packed or unpacked, everyone was expected to lend a hand—even the star aerialists.

But Jules was still on the mend from a serious blaster burn that had carved a large chunk out of his left calf. Grafts and regeneratives had restored the area so that only the closest of looks would show that there ever had been a wound there. But strength and agility were other matters. Jules had spent months conditioning the muscles, using all the knowledge of physical therapy at his disposal to bring them back to their original abilities. For the most part he had been successful, but occasionally— under severe stress—there were slight twinges.

The work was made easier by the fact that Vesa's surface gravity was only twenty-five percent of Earth normal—less than ten percent of what he was accustomed to on his home world. His movements in the bulky spacesuit were a poetry of fluid motion; he could have been born in a spacesuit for all the natural agility he displayed. There were a few times when he felt his bad leg about to give out unexpectedly under him, but Jules was able to shift his weight to the other leg in time so that nothing happened. Fizcono, he noticed, was watching his performance extra carefully, but if the foreman spotted any of these slight lapses he did not choose to mention them.

The real trouble started almost the instant the shift was over. Rask and Brownsend had spent most of the day hovering near Jules, despite his growing distaste for the two men. Every time one of the Chandakhari slipped up or made the slightest error, they would dig each other or Jules in the ribs and cast significant glances through their helmets, as if to say, "See how inept those Chandies really are?"

As soon as they were back in the changing room and had removed their helmets, Rask and Brownsend continued their jibes. Fizcono cast them a warning glance as he left to work on his reports, but they refused to acknowledge it. "Those Chandies sure are lucky Fizcono protects them," Rask sniped. "They wouldn't be able to find jobs anywhere else."

"Except maybe as stokers in the recycling plant," Brownsend agreed. "There they'd be reaching their natural level. But you can't expect really skilled work from a bunch of farmers and peasants."

Jules was watching the group of Chandakhari carefully. They were tense and doing their best to ignore the taunts —it was obvious they were used to them by now—but there was one among them who was tenser than the rest. He was quite young, not yet twenty Earth years by the look of him. His long, straight black hair hung down over his forehead almost into his eyes, and he had tried to grow a mustache that struggled to exist on his upper lip as a skinny black smudge. For the life of him, Jules could not remember the lad's name—but that was not important. More significant was the fact that the boy was about to explode with anger at the two persecutors.

Hoping to avoid a scene, Jules stepped up to Rask and Brownsend. "Farming is a lot more demanding a skill than you think it is," he began in a conciliatory tone. "I tried it once when I was younger, and had to give it up. It's a lot simpler to tote boxes than run a farm, believe me."

Brownsend looked Jules up and down, wondering what to make of this change in tack. Finally, deciding that he was bigger than the newcomer, he thought he would include him in the litany of abuse. "I'm not surprised *you* found it hard," he said. "Leave it to the runt of the litter to defend the honor of those ignorant yokels."

Jules was struggling so hard to keep his own temper at an even level that he did not notice the young Chandakhar launching himself angrily across the room at Brownsend, murder in his eyes. The lower gravity did, however, allow him time to realize what was happening and get set for action while the youth was still in the air. To Jules, the young man's body floated with excruciating slowness while the SOTE agent eyed the rest of the figures in the room and prepared for the coming battle.

Brownsend, his reflexes not as fast as Jules's, was caught by surprise at the sudden attack. He barely had time to fling his arms up in defense as the seventy-five-kilogram body crashed squarely into him, knocking him backward onto the floor. He hit with a thud that knocked the wind from his lungs, and found that the Chandakhar had a grip on his throat that was intended to keep air out of them permanently.

The other Chandakhari were as startled by their fellow's attack as Brownsend was, and they exhibited a split second of hesitation. Not so Rask, who looked as though he'd been all set for a fight. There was a wrench in his belt, one of the many tools that dangled there for the cargoman's use. Instantly it was in his hand, and his arm was upraised to deliver a blow that would smash the young man's skull.

It was at this point that Jules chose to interfere. As Rask's arm came up, Jules grabbed the wrist in an unbreakable grip and pulled down hard from the rear. Rask, his body unprepared for an attack from this new direction, flipped over backward. So slowly did he spin in the air as he came down that Jules had plenty of time to turn around, bring up his knee and deliver a staggering blow just under the man's ribs. Rask was unconscious before he even hit the floor.

Without pausing to check the results of his action, Jules turned his attention to the pair of bodies struggling on the floor. Brownsend was writhing about, trying to dislodge the young man who clung tenaciously to his throat. Spinning once more, Jules faced the two combatants and swung his right arm downward in a wide, graceful motion. Despite the fact that his movement looked casual, there was a loud smack as his fist connected with the side of the Chandakhar's head. The force of the impact knocked the youngster aside and made him release his hold on Brownsend's throat. The older man lay quietly on the floor, gulping in huge breaths of air to his oxygen-starved lungs, while the younger knelt stunned, shaking his head to clear it after the mind-numbing blow it had been dealt.

The fight *should* have ended there, with the three hot-bloods incapacitated. But just out of the corner of his eye Jules caught a flash of movement, and he whirled to face the oncoming charge of the six remaining Chandakhari. They had seen him attack their young friend and, notwithstanding the fact that he had also prevented the lad's head from getting bashed in by Rask's wrench, they felt obliged to protect their countryman from his assault.

Jules had fought six men at a time before, and in circumstances much more harrowing than this. But the fact that registered the strongest in his brain as he watched the half dozen opponents charging him was that they moved as a precision unit. By all rights, six men in a spontaneous situation like this should have been an un-coordinated mob; even with a common purpose, some of them should be duplicating their efforts while leaving several other openings free.

Instead, these Chandakhari behaved like a military drill team going through its paces. Two of them snatched at Jules' ankles, pinning them solidly together and anchoring him to the spot. Two more grabbed at his wrists, holding them straight out to the sides. A fifth grabbed Jules by the waist and, with the help of the other four, lifted the startled DesPlainian bodily off the ground. The sixth man locked the crook of his elbow tightly about Jules' neck, pulling the head back sharply and exposing his gullet.

Being held at all points as he was, Jules was totally deprived of a leverage point to use in his struggles. Had he been even the slightest bit less powerful he might have been killed on the spot. As it was, it took every iota of his supernormal strength to wrench free his right wrist from the grip of the man holding it. That breaking free unbalanced the hold his attackers had, and he dipped suddenly toward the floor.

With the speed of reflexes unique to the d'Alembert clan, Jules reached down with his now free right hand and grasped the legs of the man holding his waist. One mighty heave was sufficient to pull the man off his feet, and the entire configuration caved in. Jules lashed out with hands and feet as he found himself on the floor amid a tangle of bodies.

"What's going on here?" boomed the loud voice of Laz Fizcono from across the room.

All action ceased as the big man's words penetrated the brains of those present. The anger, the frustration, the tension that had been so explosively released was now just as quickly quelled. Every man in the room was suddenly aware that his job was on the line, and that he'd better play it cautiously.

When no one answered his question—which had been largely rhetorical, anyway—Fizcono put his hands to his hips and glared into the faces of all present. "It looks to me like a fight," he went on, "and I hate fights among people who have to work together in dangerous situations.

I want you all to hate fights, too. And just to make sure that you'll all hate fights, I'm docking everyone who was in it a full week's pay."

"But I didn't . . ." Brownsend began to rasp.

"You were in it," Fizcono said sternly, "and you couldn't have been doing it all by yourself. Nor could anyone else. We have to stop this kind of crap before someone ends up dead outside." He stopped and looked particularly at Jules. "This was a bad way to start a new job, duChamps. I expected a little better of you; frankly, I'm disappointed."

As the foreman disappeared into the corridor again, an awkward silence fell upon the changing room. Men averted their eyes guiltily, not quite daring to look at each other. As for Jules, he sat on the floor for a moment, stretching his neck and thinking about the way the Chandakhari had attacked.

CHAPTER 4

The Resurrection of Carmen Velasquez

While Jules was investigating Vesa's society from the bottom up, both d'Alemberts had agreed that Yvette should investigate it from the top down. Setting herself up as a target was potentially more dangerous, but the life she would be leading in the meantime would have its compensations. Thus, while her brother took the fastest flight possible to Vesa, Yvette d'Alembert devoted some time to building a good disguise and arranging luxury accommodations for herself on the plushest starliner heading for her destination.

"Carmen Velasquez would be perfect for this assignment, don't you think?" she'd asked her brother as they planned their respective modes of attack.

"I think all that rich living went to your head," Jules retorted. "Carmen was exactly the sort of person who *would* be missed—not a good prospective victim at all."

Yvette pondered her brother's words for a moment. On their last assignment—that of tracking down and destroying the Galaxy-wide treasonous network of Banion the Bastard, pretender to the Throne—the two of them had posed as Carlos and Carmen Velasquez, two *nouveau riche* ex-Puritans. The Velasquezes had actually been a parody of wealth, wearing outlandish costumes and throwing hundred-ruble bills around as though they'd been kopeks. Amid the subdued richness of the planet Algonia they had stood out like a supernova in a bathtub.

There had been a good reason at the time for such a broad burlesque. Banion's forces were getting closer to the day of their unleashing, and a tempting target had to be offered. With no leads at all, the d'Alemberts had had to make absolutely certain that they would be noticed. They were, of course, and the comparative small fry they caught with that net had enabled them eventually to trace down the entire organization.

But Jules was right—the old Carmen would not be the sort of victim the Vesan murderers were looking for. As flashy and funky as she was, she would make an impression even on that flashy, funky moon. Her sudden disappearance would be noticed—something the crooks were obviously trying to avoid. "Well," Yvette admitted aloud, "there *will* have to be some changes made. . . ."

And indeed there were. The old Carmen had been a madcap wife; the new was a sedate, rational widow. The old Carmen had dressed in outfits that showed as much bare skin as the local law allowed; the new wore clothes that were elegant and moderate, neither brassy nor matronly, but designed to show tastefully that there was still a beautiful woman inside them. The old Carmen had glittered from head to toe with expensive jewelry; the new, while not shunning such displays of opulence, wore her jewels one or two at a time in such a manner as to tastefully enhance, rather than clash with, her outfit.

The *Empress Irene* was one of the newest and most luxurious starliners cruising the spacelanes—the natural vehicle for a person like Carmen Velasquez to utilize on her vacation trip to Vesa. Her suite was spacious, with plush carpeting and drapes, a king-size bed and a bathtub

39

longer than she was. For her particular convenience, the rooms had even been specially rigged for ultra-grav. While the entire ship, except for certain recreation areas, was under one gee of artificial gravity, her own suite had been raised to three at her request. Since Carmen was ostensibly from Purity—a heavy-grav world settled in part by religious fanatics who broke away from Des-Plaines—her request for the higher gravity was in no way surprising.

The voyage from Earth to Vesa was to take ten days, but from the very first Yvette established herself as one of *the* people aboard. As lovely and wealthy as she was, she was constantly invited to dine at the captain's table. When word got around that she was single as well, men were lining up outside her door to escort her to dances or to offer to be her partner in some of the many shipboard activities and sports. Yvette reveled in the attention. After all, there was no law that a dangerous assignment had to be boring as well.

On the fifth day out, Yvette met up with a very charming man from the planet Largo. His name was Dak Lehman, he was an industrialist on vacation, and he was most girls' idea of a dream man. In his early thirties, he was a blend of mature sophistication and boyish enthusiasm. He knew all the social graces, and could converse with both wit and intelligence. Even more important, he knew the value of good listening. When he was with a woman she felt she had his entire attention; a flattering quality that made him the delight of all the females aboard ship.

It was only natural, then, that the two most attractive people aboard the liner should find one another and become instantly attracted. Dak took Yvette to the dinner dance that fifth night, and the beautiful SOTE agent knew she was in for a delightful evening. Dak let her do most of the talking during the meal, which Yvette didn't mind —it gave her a good opportunity to practice her background story and polish it up for Vesa. She let her date know that she was a widow at twenty-nine, but that her husband had left her exceedingly wealthy. The mining operations that they had started together were now in the

40

hands of an efficient and honest business manager, so poor Carmen had nothing else to do but travel around and enjoy herself. It was a carefully crafted story, designed to let would-be murderers know that her disappearance would cause few ripples in the stream of life.

Dak listened sympathetically as she talked. "You look awfully young to be a widow," he said when she'd finished.

"I didn't know they'd set an age limit. Poor Carlos was buried under a rockfall in one of our mines. His body was never recovered." Yvette allowed herself a languid sigh.

"I still find it hard to believe that someone as worldly and sophisticated as you could have come from Purity. I'd always heard that they were . . . well. . . ."

"Try, 'stuffy,' 'provincial' or 'boring.' Most fanatics are. I was raised that way myself, and I still surprise myself with the traces every so often. Fortunately, money can teach you a lot of things in a hurry—or at least buy you the teachers. Carlos and I decided we enjoyed life too much to coop ourselves up with that Puritanical existence, so we left for Earth seven years ago." She sniffed. "Poor Carlos. To have died so young, without knowing so many of the pleasures."

At this point the orchestra began to play. Dak invited her out onto the dance floor, and Yvette accepted happily. Both of them, it turned out, were superb dancers, their bodies melding into one smooth movement that swayed with the rhythm of the music. Yvette's body tingled as it pressed ever closer to Dak's. This was certainly one charming man, the sort a woman could easily fall in love with.

When the dance ended, Dak guided Yvette out of the ballroom and into the adjoining chamber known as the Cosmos Room. This was an open room twenty meters across with a domed ceiling that rose ten meters up over the heads of the people inside. The room was kept permanently darkened while a kaleidoscope of pinpoint lights played across the dome, giving it the appearance of a psychedelic planetarium. Occasionally the magnified picture of a nebula or foreign galaxy would appear, swooping downwards onto the populace like a descending hawk.

41

Ostensibly the Cosmos Room was designed for meditation on the vastness of the Universe; in point of fact, it served to spur the development of shipboard liaisons that were part of a starliner's legendary appeal to romantics of both sexes.

Dak led Yvette to the handrailing along one wall and together they watched the light show play across the dome for several minutes. It was Yvette who broke the silence. "I've spent the entire evening so far talking about myself," she said. "How about letting me know a little bit about you? Who is this fascinating fellow named Dak Lehman?"

Her date was strangely silent for a long moment, which Yvette found quite uncharacteristic. Dak was never pressed for an answer in conversation. Yvette was about to comment jokingly on his hesitation when she felt a strange prickly sensation on the back of her neck. Someone was watching her; her agent's instinct was definite on that point. Casually she shifted her body around so that she could look in the direction of the stare without appearing to notice it. As her eyes peered through the darkness of the room she could make out the shapes of two men. One was of normal height but slightly portly, the other was tall and lanky. She couldn't make out much else in this poor light, but they were definitely watching her. That was all they seemed interested in for now, so Yvette filed the information away in her mind for later evaluation and turned her attention back to Dak. She kept checking the watchers every few minutes, though, to make sure they weren't up to something.

Dak had finally gotten around to answering her question. Yvette laid a hand gently over his wrist as he spoke. "Oh, I'm not anybody too important, really. My father ran a small voicewriter manufacturing company on Largo. When I inherited it I expanded the operation until we became the largest business machine company in that sector of space. We've recently branched out still further into computers, and we're doing fantastically well there, too. I decided to get away from home for a while, before too much success did me in. It can be pretty heady wine, but the social atmosphere was getting rather stifling. I'm

42

hoping Vesa will change that; I hear very few people ever win anything there. It'll be a refreshing difference."

"And there aren't any women in your life?"

Again, that slight pause. "No, no, not at present. I've always been too busy to let anything really permanent develop. Sort of married to my work, you might say."

Yvette had put her hand on his wrist for a reason. As sensitive as she was she could act as a human lie detector, picking up the small changes in pulse rate, the minute tensions in the muscles that occurred when a person was ill at ease with what he was saying. It was a trick she had learned years ago from her Uncle Marcel, the Circus' magician, to whom it was an indispensable part of his mentalist act.

What she'd learned from "reading" Dak's wrist annoyed her. He did not seem to be directly lying, but at the same time he was steering his way very carefully between the pillars of the truth. Not a single thing he'd said had been completely accurate. This disturbed her, for she'd begun to find herself caring for him quite a bit.

From back in the ballroom the orchestra had struck up another dance tune. Yvette suddenly found herself impatient with this time and place. "Let's go back and dance some more," she said, taking her date firmly by the hand and leading him in the direction of the dance floor. He offered no resistance whatsoever.

The two watchers vanished into the shadows as she moved back toward the ballroom, and that disturbed her even more. *Why were they watching me?* she wondered. *Do they have anything to do with this case? But they couldn't have broken my cover this quickly!*

Questions swarmed around her mind all evening, refus-ing to let her simply enjoy herself.

The next five days went by rapidly. For the most part they were very relaxing, with Yvette spending most of her time in Dak's company. They conversed in trivial matters, childhood experiences and gossip about the activities of their fellow passengers. They played at the shipboard sports, and Yvette had to be supercareful not to let her physical talents show too much. Their favorite pastime was "freeswimming" in the zero gee room, a sport far superior to water swimming for several reasons: it could be done in three dimensions without the heavy resistance of water, there was no drying off to do afterwards, no special clothing to wear—in fact, freeswimming was usually done nude—and there was absolutely no fear of drowning.

Yvette was used to freefall, having been traveling through space with the Circus since she was a baby, but she rarely had the pleasure of enjoying it in a large room where she could be free to soar and do acrobatics to her heart's content. She really came alive while freeswimming, and her exuberance infected all those around her. She twisted and spun and somersaulted in the air to the applause of her fellow passengers—who had no idea they were watching the premiere aerialiste in the Galaxy.

"You certainly do that well," Dak remarked one time as his eyes admiringly tracked over Yvette's lovely, svelte body.

Yvette flashed him her warmest smile. "Physical fitness has always been a passion of mine. My body is my home and I have only the one—I want to take care of it as best I can." She spent the rest of that day teaching Dak the basics of her art. He was an apt pupil, and after only a couple of hours they were performing together in an acceptable, if not totally polished, manner.

The only thing that marred the blissful perfection of those last few days was the continued presence of those two shadowy watchers. At first, Yvette noticed them only when she was together with Dak—a pair of indistinct forms observing them discreetly from a vantage point where they themselves could only barely be seen. But after a while, as her relationship with Dak deepened, one or the other of them was with her almost constantly.

For convenience' sake, she named the tall one Gaspard and the fat one Murgatroyd, and tried every trick she knew to bring them out into the open—to no avail. She tried ducking around corners and doubling back on them, but they were wise to that trick and refused to be caught. She tried mingling in large crowds and open rooms, but they were equally adept at mingling and remained hidden

44

while watching her. She was able to shake them off her trail temporarily several times, but on a closed ship there were only so many places she could go and they always picked her up again within a couple of hours.

Who are they? she found herself wondering more and more. *They're damned good, I'll give them credit for that. Could they be a part of the conspiracy I'm here to investigate? There's no evidence to suggest that the mob has advance scouts on the ships coming into Vesa—but that doesn't mean they don't. Whoever they are, they give me purple fits.*

It was now the last night of the voyage. Tomorrow the *Empress Irene* would be docking on Vesa and Yvette's real work would begin; but as for tonight, she just wanted to relax and enjoy herself. She and Dak had a marvelous dinner and their conversation was freer than any they'd had before. A couple of times Yvette saw a dark thought pass behind her date's eyes and he almost came out and told her what it was. But something made him hold back, and he would change the subject abruptly. Yvette, feeling it was not her place to pry, said nothing.

After dinner they walked slowly about the ship, arms around each other's waists, not saying much of anything. When they came to the elevator tube where they would have to part to go to their respective suites, Dak invited her to come to his for the night instead. Yvette hesitated, then turned him down politely, citing her recent widowhood as an excuse. "As I said, occasionally my Puritan upbringing comes through and surprises even me. Your offer is tempting, but Carlos' death was so recent. . . ." She let her voice trail off wistfully.

"I understand," Dak said softly. He turned toward her, gazing down into her beautiful face, and both his arms wrapped around her. Their bodies were pressed together for a silent sensual minute before he spoke again. "I'm usually so well spoken that when a genuine emotion comes my way I sometimes get choked up. This is one of those times. I know there's a mystique about shipboard romances, and it's something I've been consciously fighting —but I've lost. Carmen, I think I'm in love with you. Will you marry me?"

45

Yvette found herself suddenly with tears in her eyes. "Your speechlessness must be contagious," she stammered. "The only thing that comes to my mind is the old cliché that this is all so sudden. I don't know what to think. You deserve a better answer than that, I know, but that's all I can give you at the moment."

Dak shrugged. "I'm not expecting an answer tonight. Maybe in the cold light of morning on Vesa we'll think how silly we were to mistake desire for love. Let's both just think about it for a while, shall we?"

"I can't think of a pleasanter subject to think about," Yvette replied.

The two stood by the elevator tube for a long minute with their bodies held closely together, luxuriating in the feel of one another's warmth. Then Dak bent his head down to hers and their lips met in a passionate kiss.

Yvette's whole body was still tingling from that kiss as she went up the tube and then made her way down the long corridor to her suite. Her mind was in a pleasant haze of confusion brought on by a conflict between her emotions and her rational mind. Her feelings were telling her that here at last was a man she could love. She was twenty-nine years old and still single; among the prolific d'Alembert clan that was considered slightly unusual. She had had her share of romantic entanglements, but never before had the magic spark burned so brightly as now. Dak Lehman was handsome, intelligent, charming, pleasant, wealthy, available, and in love with her. The combination couldn't get more perfect than that. It didn't matter that her father, besides managing the Circus, was also the Duke of the entire planet of DesPlaines and that she herself was a Lady of the Realm. There was no stigma attached to marrying a commoner; in some circles, in fact, it was actively encouraged.

The one fact she could not ignore, however, was that Dak Lehman was not a DesPlainian. It was not chauvinism but practicality that made that point so important. Dak's home planet of Largo had a surface gravity approximately equal to Earth's, while Yvette came from a world three times as strong. He could never live com-

46

fortably on her home world; even in peak physical condition as he was now, he would be largely incapacitated. In ten, twenty, thirty years he would become a hopeless cripple.

Yvette would be able to tolerate the low gravity of other worlds much better, but there would still be complications. People from high-grav worlds tended to develop bone diseases when they moved permanently to smaller ones. She herself could wind up an arthritic cripple—a fate she didn't relish. Plus, she would have to go into a self-imposed exile from all the friends and family she felt closest to.

There was the question, too, of relative strength. She had had to be very careful thus far in their relationship not to use her full strength. Even in the midst of their most passionate embrace she had had to hold off using her power, for fear of cracking several of his ribs. If they were to be married she would be living with that fear constantly, afraid to let herself go completely because she might hurt or even kill him. It was this collection of doubts that tempered her ecstasy as she fished in her purse to find her key.

But I do love him, she realized.

As she pulled the magnetic key from her purse and was about to run it over the surface of the door's lock, she noticed a light shining out from under the doorframe. She distinctly remembered turning out the lights as she'd left her room four hours ago . . . and these lights were not automatically timed to go on by themselves.

Instantly all thoughts of Dak Lehman were banished from her mind and she was once again Yvette d'Alembert, top agent for the Service of the Empire. Business was at hand. Some person or persons had broken into her room, had turned on a light and had left it on. It could be a simple burglary and the thief may have departed hours ago, but she could not afford to take that chance. Searching back through her memory, she suddenly realized one reason why this evening had seemed so carefree—her two menacing shadows had not been following her. It had perplexed her slightly at first, but she had forgotten it in the delightful evening that followed. Now it was all suddenly clear. They had not followed her because they were setting an ambush in her own room.

Yvette was glad she had not accepted Dak's proposition. She'd been getting very nervous about these two faceless ones for some time now, but had been unable to initiate action. Now it was finally they who were starting something, and Yvette resolved to be the one to finish it.

Her analytical mind raced, deciding what strategy she should take. The hall was normally quiet and she had made no attempt to silence her footsteps, so Gaspard and Murgatroyd would know she was presently standing outside the door. They would be taking no chances—their guns would be trained on the door to shoot her the instant she opened it. Blasters or stunners, it would make no difference; they would be trying to incapacitate her somehow.

But they would be aiming at a target standing in the doorway, because that was the normal way people entered a room. They would probably aim fairly low— waist height or lower—to ensure a hit. But there might be another way to enter a room. . . .

Looking quickly around, Yvette spotted what she wanted. All starliners were equipped with series of handholds for emergency use in case their artificial gravity failed. These had been made to blend in with the decor, but they were there and would be sturdy enough for what she had in mind. She fixed in her mind the position of the one just above her door and braced herself for action.

She rubbed the magnetic key across the surface of the lock, but did not stick around to await the results. Instead, she leaped for the handhold above her door. As the door slid silently open, she could hear the low buzzing of stun-guns discharging, firing at the spot where she should by all rights have been standing. Instead, the beams passed harmlessly through the air and vibrated against the opposite wall of the corridor.

Yvette grabbed the handhold firmly and used it as a pivot point. Taking advantage of the forward momentum of her leap, she swung her legs forward and to the side, through the upper half of the portal, and landed out of the line of fire next to a chair. As she was descending, she noted that her ambushers had turned the gravity in her room back down to one gee, obviously for their own convenience. What they did not realize was that the lower gravity would also make it easier for her to fight them.

The two men had stationed themselves three meters apart against the far wall and were aiming at the doorway to catch her in a vee crossfire. Yvette's brain assimilated that knowledge in a fraction of a second and plotted her next move accordingly. She did not pause as she landed, but instead bent her legs under her as springs, using the force of her impact as the impetus for another leap. She flew across the room toward the man she'd name Murgatroyd, twisting catlike in midair as she did so; by the time she reached him, her feet were in front of her to cushion her landing. At the same time her right hand lashed out sideways and the edge of it delivered a vicious blow to the side of the man's neck. Had she not deliberately pulled the punch at the last second the neck would have snapped; as it was, Murgatroyd reeled and fell unconscious to the floor while Yvette, in one fluid motion, spun herself around and launched herself at the other gunman.

This fellow was the one she'd called Gaspard, and his reflexes were good. Yvette's attack on his companion had given him the split second he needed to recover from the surprise of her entrance and begin to turn in her direction. Even so, his reflexes were no match for those of a DesPlainian in peak condition.

Just as he swiveled and brought his gun up level to fire, Yvette was on top of him, seventy kilograms of infuriated mass. The impact of her body knocked them both to the ground, and a quick jab of her stiffened fingers just under his ribcage knocked the air out of his lungs and the fight out of his spirit.

As the second man went limp, Yvette breathed a small sigh of relief and got to her feet. A sudden motion caught her eye at the very limit of her peripheral vision, but before she could turn to see what it was she heard the buzzing of a stun-gun. Paralysis numbed her body and she fell, limp-boned, face forward onto the carpeting.

The hidden gunman must have used a number one setting on his stunner, the minimum possible, because Yvette did not lose consciousness. All that happened was that her voluntary muscles refused to obey her strenuous demands to act, leaving her lying helpless in the middle of the floor. The fact that her assailant had used so low a setting was encouraging—he could just as easily have killed her—but it was little consolation to her at this particular moment.

Yvette was furious at herself for having been so stupid. Just because she had only seen two followers before didn't mean that there only *were* two. She had allowed her own self-confidence to lure her into a false assumption; she should never have relaxed her guard until she'd checked the room thoroughly to make sure there were no other attackers hiding in it. In the deadly game of espionage, a player was usually allowed only one mistake, because one was usually fatal. Yvette was praying that would not be the case this time, and she swore she would never make such a stupid blunder again.

As she lay there she could hear the approaching footsteps of the person who'd shot her. She could not turn her head to see, but soon a pair of men's shoes stepped into her field of vision. "You are to be congratulated, Gospozha Velasquez; you fought better than anyone would have expected. We underestimated you, and that's something I hate to do. Rest assured, that will not happen again.

"I should begin, I suppose, by telling you that we mean you no harm personally. That sounds ludicrous in view of our ambush, I know, but all our stunners were set on one. We merely wanted to have a talk with you without your interrupting or objecting. We are reasonable men."

The voice paused as the stranger took one step backwards and sat down on the edge of her bed. "We've noticed, in the last couple of days, that you've taken an inordinate interest in Gospodin Lehman. As it turns out, we also have an interest in Gospodin Lehman, and we

50

become—how shall I say it?—jealous when other people enter the picture. We would strongly prefer it, Gospozha Velasquez, if you would refrain from seeing Gospodin Lehman again. We know how these shipboard romances can happen—as I said, we are reasonable men—and if you never see Gospodin Lehman again you will never see us again, either.

"You are about to vacation on Vesa, one of the Galaxy's greatest playgrounds. There will be more than ample opportunity to forget all about Gospodin Lehman. You are a very attractive woman, Gospozha Velasquez, and I have no doubt there will be scores of handsome men throwing themselves at your feet to compensate for the one you must give up. You are also an intelligent woman, which is why I will not belabor the point of how upset my friends and I would be if you should disregard our suggestions."

The man stood up again and came over to Gaspard. The tall man had not been knocked completely unconscious by Yvette's blow—she had been meaning to question him about his reasons for following her—and had been quietly retching while his comrade was speaking. Now he was slowly picking himself up, aided by his friend. Together, the two of them went over and inspected Murgatroyd, who was still out cold.

Picking up their fallen companion, the two men headed for the door. As they stopped on the threshold, the one who had done all the talking said, "Again, I offer our apologies for the disturbance, Gospozha Velasquez. We hope you have a pleasant vacation on Vesa."

By the time the effects of the stunner wore off some ten minutes later it would be impossible to track down the men. Yvette had to settle for lying awake in her bed all night, staring up at the darkened ceiling and planning exactly what she would do to that trio the next time she ran into them.

CHAPTER 5

Accidents

Jules' second day at work on Vesa was much calmer than the first. The air was very quiet; even people who hadn't participated in the previous day's brawl were walking on eggshells, afraid to set off the dynamite that they knew instinctively was still buried in the personalities of the men involved. A fragile tension buzzed through the air like a noisy fly uncertain where to light.

Adding to the problem was the fact that the crew was shorthanded today. Brownsend did not show up for work, and a quick call to his apartment by Fizcono yielded no results. "Probably nursing his wounds," the big man muttered. "He didn't look so good when he went home yesterday. He'd better be back tomorrow, though, or he's fired. I won't tolerate jackdandles around here."

Rask went around sullenly, not speaking more than a couple of words to anyone as he suited up. It was obvious he felt unfairly punished for the fracas—after all, it had been the Chandakhari who had attacked first; he'd just tried to protect his friend, and had been docked a week's pay for it. The injustice of it all grated harshly on his ego.

The Chandakhari, in turn, were even more stand-offish, more clique-ish, more withdrawn from the other workers. The young man who'd begun the actual fighting—Jules remembered now that his name was Radapur—stood aloof and proud, glaring occasionally across at Rask with a semi-sneer across his lips.

Jules was in the worst position of all, because nobody was quite sure where he stood on the matter. During the fight he had come to the aid of both sides, and had earned enmity each way. No one could bring himself to completely trust this newcomer, and so he became the outcast for the day.

That was all just as well as far as he was concerned,

because he had a good deal of thinking to do. He had gone out yesterday after work, checking out the bars in the shadier portions of the underground city. He had not been able to cover it all in one night, of course; the settlement that was Vesa comprised millions of square kilometers of caverns and corridors, with more being added all the time as the moon's wealth grew. But even though he'd just seen a tiny fraction of the life here, a picture was beginning to emerge that puzzled him greatly.

Vesa had quite a scandalous reputation throughout the Galaxy as a gambler's haven, a world of iniquity, where anything goes as long as the customer has enough rubles to pay the price. Based on this reputation, Jules had expected to find the private life on Vesa equally lascivious and wild. Instead, he found it just the reverse. The permanent inhabitants of Vesa were, on the whole, a clean-living bunch. The handful of bars he visited were orderly and sedate, with little raucous laughter and no fights breaking out at an instant's notice. There were the usual drunks and *dyevkas*, but they seemed somehow set apart from the run of the ordinary people.

Jules saw little evidence, on that quick skim, of any major corruption, let alone an enormous conspiracy to kill tourists. How could so quiet and civilized a people be responsible for what all the evidence indicated was happening?

On the other hand, there was still the fascinating development of what happened during the fight. Those Chandakhari had reacted like a well-rehearsed fighting unit. Each man had known exactly where to go and what to do when the trouble started. That was not the sort of thing he would expect of a group of farm peasants, or even dockmen used to barroom brawls. There was a military precision to their actions that was frightening. The Chandakhari would, Jules decided, bear closer inspection.

The first part of the day went evenly enough, even if the tension among the work crew was thick enough to cut with a butter knife. Shortly after the lunch break, though, a minor explosion occurred. One of the Chandakhari was using his crane to swing a cargo section out of a ship's hold and onto the flatbed carrier. It was Rask's assignment to clear the space for the section and guide it home, while others of the workers helped steady the box. Somehow a signal was missed on one side or another, and the box went tumbling out of control from the crane. It landed with a noiseless thud that jarred the soles of everyone's feet, not on the carrier but on the floor of the crater itself. The impact was more than the container was built to withstand, and it smashed open, scattering its contents all over the airless surface.

Rask's anger flared like a supernova. "You filthy little kulyak!" he screamed over the radio circuits for all the men to hear. "You missed my mark on purpose!"

The Chandakhar crane operator, a man named Forakhi, did not take kindly to being compared with one of the least sanitary animals of the Galaxy, and yelled something back in his own native tongue. It must have been pretty vile, because the other Chandakhari seemed to wither at its usage. Then the crane man continued, "I didn't miss your mark—you deliberately gave me the wrong one so that I would drop the box."

"Are you calling me a liar?" Rask roared.

Suddenly the presence of Laz Fizcono had insinuated itself between the two arguing men, and that was a presence to be reckoned with. "I don't want to hear any more talk of things being done intentionally," the big man bellowed, drowning out the noises Forakhi and Rask were making. "I was watching it all very closely, and it was an accident pure and simple. We're all tense today; we'll have to try harder to avoid mistakes."

He turned to look at the cargo that had spilled over the floor of the crater. The ruined container had been filled with lettuce, tens of thousands of heads that now now lay ruined all around the carrier. Since lettuce is composed mostly of water, the harsh glare of Vesa's sunlight and the open vacuum combined to sizzle all the juices out of the scattered heads and turn them almost instantly into disgusting lumps of brownish green slime.

"What we need to do right now," the forman continued, "is get this mess cleaned up so that we can get on with our work." He turned to Jules. "DuChamps, I want you, Hastings, Ktobu and Hassahman to clear out the area. Get rid of this stuff before it gets fried completely to the ground. Me, I've got to go fill out the insurance forms on this, and that always gives me a headache. The rest of you men can continue with what you were doing; an accident is no excuse to stop working."

Jules and his three designated coworkers set about their new task at once. Racing back to the hangar where equipment was stored, they located the special unit they needed and drove it out to the site of the mishap. This machine, called the "scraper," was essentially a tractor with a sharp-edged flattened front that acted as a huge dustpan. As it drove forward it scraped the frying lettuce heads off the smooth ground and, when enough had been collected, it lifted them over the heads of the crew and deposited them in a large bin. Jules and Ktobu went ahead of the machine, helping to guide the refuse into it while Hassahman drove and Hastings tamped down the bin after every filling.

"What do we do with all this garbage once we pick it up?" Jules wondered aloud. "Does it just get burned, or what?"

Ktobu shook his head. "Can't afford to waste it like that. The recycling center comes and picks up the bin."

Once Ktobu pointed out the obvious, the solution made eminent sense to Jules. Vesa, as an airless moon, was a closed society. There were probably small hydroponic gardens scattered about growing a small percentage of the food consumed here, but most of it had to be imported from Chandakha and elsewhere. All organic matter was potentially edible, and none could be allowed to be wasted. In order to cut down on the amount of importation, there would have to be a recycling plant to sort through the organic refuse and salvage as much of it as possible for future use. All airless worlds had such systems, but Jules had not visited too many and had never given the matter close consideration before now.

It took the rest of that work shift and a half hour of overtime besides to clean up the mess that had been made. Fizcono, efficient as ever, had put in an order for a truck from the recycling plant, and it arrived just at the time Jules and his crew brought the scraper with its bin filled to overflowing back to the hangar. The white-clad recycler attendants went silently about their business of transferring the refuse from the bin to their truck, then drove off with hardly a word. "Are they always that brusque?" Jules asked Fizcono.

The big man nodded. "It's almost a caste situation," he explained. "The caste system was officially ended long before Chandakha was settled, but social taboos sometimes take a very long time to die, especially among such traditionalist people. Because the workers at the recycling plant handle wastes and dead matter, they're ritually unclean and are shunned by most of the rest of society. People just prefer not to have too much to do with them." He shrugged his massive shoulders. "Can't say I blame 'em much, either. It's a pretty disgusting occupation, once you think about it."

As soon as Jules clocked out he went back to his cheap hotel room, changed his clothes and went out for another night of barhopping. The situation was much as he had found it the night before—entirely too quiet. He did overhear a few conversations indicating that there was some criminal activity on the moon, but it was of a routine sort: drugs, theft, prostitution and extortion. The local police were—or should be—able to keep that under control; Jules was looking for bigger game. And it was nowhere to be found.

I'll have to try a new direction, he thought wearily as he came home and climbed into his bed. *There's got to be a hook to this affair somehow. Thirty-five people a day are vanishing. There's got to be an organization around doing it—and if there is, they'll have to surface somewhere.*

He fell asleep quickly, but got little rest that night; dreams of indeterminate murders tossed him all about the bed.

It was a chore just to drag himself to work the next day. His lack of success at finding clues about the conspiracy was depressing him, and the thought of another

56

eight hours on the job sandwiched between two warring factions only added to the feeling of malaise. He toyed with the idea of dropping the job and spending all his time investigating; he certainly didn't need the money, and the hours spent at the dock were detracting from both his time and his stamina for his real work. But, attractive as that idea was, he let it go past with only a sigh of regret. Being a secret agent, he knew, was ninety-nine percent legwork. He needed a basic identity in case he got into trouble, and he shouldn't be letting the glamor of the field go to his head. This dull job, too, came with the territory.

He arrived five minutes late, and almost everyone else was suited up. As he quickly scurried into his own space-suit, he looked around and noticed that they were two hands short today—not only was Brownsend still absent, but so was Rask. "Where is everybody?" he asked.

"There's still no word from Brownsend," Fizcono growled. Clearly he was not happy at having to work shorthanded. "I'm putting him on suspension for now and requisitioning a new hand from one of the other teams until he either comes back or we replace him permanently." The tone of his voice made it plain that he considered the latter possibility preferable.

"As for Rask," the foreman went on, "I don't know exactly where he is. His suit's gone from his locker, which means he might have gone outside early. That's not like him at all; he's competent, but doesn't have that much initiative. I've tried raising him on the radio, but he doesn't answer, so your guess is as good as mine as to where he is." The big man shook his head. "Don't you go temperamental on me too, duChamps, or I'll have a nervous breakdown."

The new man that Fizcono had requisitioned would not be able to join them until later in the shift, so the work crew went out onto the field two short. As usual, the Chandakhari stayed in a group by themselves, talking but little and being very introspective. They walked to the mobile crane that was their particular specialty and set out across the open crater toward the ship they were currently working on. Jules, Fizcono and the rest followed slightly behind in the flatbed carrier that was to hold the unloaded cargo.

Jules had let his mind go pleasantly blank as a relaxation technique during the mildly jostling ride, but suddenly a movement from the right brought his attention back to full alert. From behind two nearby ships, the small scraper suddenly darted out at full speed and launched itself toward the mobile crane. It was only traveling at twenty kilometers an hour, hardly a breakneck pace, but even so it was lighter and more maneuverable than the vehicle it was approaching.

Fizcono spotted the scraper at almost the same instant Jules did. "What in hell's going on out there?" he exclaimed.

Jules' sharp eyes had focused on the driver of the vehicle. "It's Rask," he said curtly. "I think he's going to ram the crane."

The words that burst from Fizcono's lips were in a slang peculiar to spacemen and dockworkers, and they expressed his displeasure in particularly graphic terms that would have burned the ears off more sensitive listeners. Jules was familiar with this brand of swearing, so it wouldn't have bothered him even if he'd been listening —which he wasn't. He was never one who could sit idly by and watch something happen; even as he was telling Fizcono what Rask was intending, he had started into action.

The crane was about ten meters ahead of the carrier on which the SOTE agent had been riding. With a slight running start, Jules leaped from the front edge of his vehicle toward the crane. His spring had been carefully gauged to utilize Vesa's low gravity to the fullest extent. The arc of his flight was a low, flat one, because he knew that the higher he went, the longer it would take him to come down and the further the crane would have traveled in the meantime. Even so, it seemed to take forever to his speeded-up senses before he approached the crane; objects fell much more slowly on Vesa.

While still along his arc he called out over the radio, "Everybody off the crane! Rask means business." At the same time, he twisted his body around in a quick acrobatic maneuver so that he would land on the crane feet first. And, while his attention was on his landing spot, he nonetheless had time to give a couple of quick glances to see what the scraper was doing.

Rask was driving the smaller vehicle in a most uneven manner. While there was no question of what its target was, the course it was taking weaved along the floor of the crater as though the driver had only partial control. Its motion was also slightly uneven, accelerating in a series of rapid jerks rather than a smooth pace.

That didn't matter. The scraper would still strike the crane with an impact that would cause major damage. And in the vacuum on the surface of Vesa, any accident could be fatal.

The crane stopped moving shortly before Jules reached it, as the Chandakhari aboard realized what was happening. After an initial moment of surprise, they reacted in accordance with Jules' suggestion, clambering off the crane as quickly as they could. Being in suits made it both difficult and dangerous, for quick movement around machinery could easily lead to a tear in the material, which in turn led to instant death. Still, Jules was encouraged and relieved to see just how fast they could move.

Jules landed with his knees bent to cushion the impact and grabbed at a nearby strut to stabilize himself. Then, with the momentum of his leap dispersed, he ran forward to the crane's cab and took the controls.

Rask was coming broadside at the crane for maximum impact. There was no way a crash could be avoided— the crane moved entirely too slow to dodge—but it was Jules' plan to try to turn the big crane through as large an angle as possible. The collision with the scraper would not be as catastrophic if the angle of impact were less than ninety degrees.

There was no sound on the airless surface of Vesa, but the noise of the gears grinding was very strong in Jules' imagination as he pushed hard at the controls. Rask's scraper was only a couple dozen meters away and closing the distance rapidly. The caterpillar treads of the crane shuddered as Jules forced them beyond their level of tolerance. Five, ten degrees the crane turned, and then it was too late. The scraper struck the side of the crane with the full force of its twenty-metric-ton mass.

Jules abandoned his position the instant before the crash occurred—he had no intention of being tossed around inside the cab and possibly having his spacesuit ripped. He was out the open door and standing on the side of the crane when the impact happened. The force of the collision transmitted itself through his feet and jarred his whole body. His head was so badly shaken that his teeth threatened to break loose and roll around in his mouth like dice on a gaming table. A sudden stab of pain lanced through his left leg just below the knee, where it was still recovering from its previous injury; Jules winced as the leg buckled slightly under him, and he grabbed a nearby strut for support.

As Rask's vehicle had hit the crane, he had activated the lift mechanism of the scraper blade, hoping to be able to overturn the larger machine. The crane rocked and trembled, and Jules was afraid for one instant that Rask might actually accomplish his goal; but the crane was simply too massive, and after a couple of seconds Rask abandoned that effort in favor of new mayhem.

Radapur, the young Chandakhar who had started the fight two days ago, had jumped away from the crane with the rest of his colleagues, and was now by himself on foot some fifteen meters away. Rask saw this and, backing away from the crane, he propelled his scraper in the direction of the lone Chandakhar.

Judging from the relative positions, Jules realized that there was no way anyone else could reach Radapur before Rask's scraper did. He would have to act on his own to save the lad. He tried to yell out a warning, but by this time the radio band was so full of yelling and epithets that no individual voices could be heard. Giving his left leg a quick test, he decided it was ready enough for action, so he braced himself to move once more.

Above and in front of him, some twenty-five meters off the ground, dangled the sky hook of the crane. Jules took a slight running start and, with legs curled under him like tightly coiled springs, he leaped upward for it.

Even considering Vesa's light gravity it would have been an impossible feat for anyone from an Earthlike world—but Jules was a DesPlainian and trained in the expert use of his physical abilities. Centuries of genetic adaptation and a lifetime of physical conditioning were implied in the force of his leap, and he made it with energy to spare.

He grabbed at the hook as he would a trapeze, and his forward momentum caused it to sway a bit. By leaning his body in the proper direction he was able to increase the swing slightly, although the hook was far more massive than any trapeze he'd even worked with. Slowly, very slowly, his pendulum was making longer and longer swings, building up the momentum he would need for one more leap.

Down on the ground, the scraper was closing in on Radapur. Slow as that vehicle was, it could still outrun a man. The young Chandakhar was using a stall tactic of leaping high into the air to get out of the machine's path, but that tactic could only be used for so long, because he would come down so slowly that Rask had time to position himself closer to the landing spot. It would only be a matter of a few seconds before the maddened driver flattened his quarry.

The hook he was riding was now swinging to Jules' satisfaction. Holding his timing until just the proper moment on the downswing, Jules let go of his perch and soared out over the empty crater toward the moving scraper. His aim had to be exceedingly accurate, since he was not working in an atmosphere that would let him make minor course corrections by adjusting his body position for variable air resistance.

Rask was apparently tiring of his hit-and-run game with Radapur, now, for he had stopped his vehicle and was standing up, pulling a blaster from his belt. He fired off a couple of bolts in Radapur's direction, but missed by wide margins. This erratic firing, coupled with Rask's earlier insane driving, led Jules to the inescapable conclusion that the man was either drunk or drugged.

Rask's stopping the scraper threw off Jules' calculations slightly, and his downward descent was a little forward of the mark. As he came down over Rask's head, though, the SOTE agent managed to kick out with his right foot and knock the blaster from the man's hand. The gun went sailing through the airless sky to land harmlessly on the ground some fifteen meters away.

Jules came down two meters in front of the scraper and rolled, being extremely careful to take the brunt of the shock on the tough parts of his suit—gloves and boots. Springing once more to his feet, he spun lightly around to face his antagonist.

Most of the yelling over the communications band had died down now, and Jules could make out Rask's voice. The man was ranting away at the top of his lungs. ". . . murderers, all of them. You must be one, too. You all killed Brownsend." Then he launched himself at Jules.

The circus star easily sidestepped the oncoming body and grabbed it as it went by. Flinging it around with one hand like a rag doll, he pulled back with his other hand and landed a closed-fist blow right under Rask's ribs. The man's eyes bugged out inside his helmet and air was forced from his lungs. His body went limp as all the fight apparently drained out of him.

Jules lowered Rask's body gently to the ground and sat straddling him. "What's gotten into you, anyhow?" he asked angrily. "I want an explanation for this."

The defeated man gasped several times like a fish out of water before he could speak again. Finally he got enough air in his lungs to say, "They killed him! Those damned Chandies killed him!"

"Killed who?"

"Brownsend. I went to his apartment last night. There was no trace of him or his things. Landlord said he just left a note saying he was leaving, but I know better. Those drapping Chandies killed him and cleaned him out to cover it up. They never did like him. I'll kill them all, every last drapping one of them!" Rask started struggling again, but Jules held the man's arms tightly to his sides and thought.

Rask's hypothesis struck a very surprising note. What he was describing seemed to be the *modus operandi* of the very gang Jules had been sent here to investigate.

Could it be that he'd stumbled on the gang totally by accident?

But even as he thought that, he could see that it was not the whole picture. The seven Chandakhari worked an eight-hour shift here. Assuming they spent another eight hours on such necessities as eating and sleeping, that meant they would have to be killing the average thirty-five people a day in only another eight hours. A rampage of death like that could not be missed even by the tourists, let alone the police. No, the seven Chandakhari working here were not the entire group he was after.

On the other hand, any doubts he had about their being involved were rapidly evaporating. He remembered back to the fight that had taken place two days ago and recalled how impressed he had been with their coordination. That they were a well-drilled team he had no doubts at all. They had almost been able to kill him, despite his considerable skills. These were not innocent farmers and dockhands—not at all.

So intent was Jules in his thoughts that Rask was able to catch him by surprise. With a burst of strength that only a madman could muster, he gave one violent jerk that bucked Jules off his body, scrambled to his feet and began racing off in the direction of his fallen blaster. The SOTE agent recovered his balance quickly and started after him, but was too late to avert the tragedy that was coming up.

The Chandakhari had formed as a group by now and interposed themselves between Rask and his gun. He hit their lines like a maniac, arms waving madly in all directions. They withstood his assault, grabbing for his limbs and immobilizing them by pinning them to his body. Then, even as he struggled furiously against their grip on him, the Chandakhari picked him up bodily and ran him over toward the scraper. With cold fury they rammed him solidly into the machine.

Rask howled, a scream that would have curdled molten lead, as a large section was ripped away from his space-suit. Jules instinctively brought his hands up to cover his ears, even though his head was solidly encased inside his helmet. The dying man's shriek pierced like an arrow through Jules' brain. It vanished quickly, though, and was replaced by a few sucking sounds as the air whooshed out of Rask's suit. Then silence.

As Jules reached them, the Chandakhari slowly lowered Rask's lifeless body to the ground. Jules looked around the group at the faces within the helmets, and saw not the slightest trace of remorse in any of them.

CHAPTER 6

Vesa Vice

When the *Empress Irene* docked on Vesa, Yvette was too busy packing up her luggage and supervising its removal from the ship to look for Dak Lehman. She had gotten little sleep that night, intent as she was on thinking about the attack in her suite. She was able to come to no conclusion whatsoever about the men who'd ambushed her. There was the possibility that they were some sort of advance scouts for the murderous conspiracy she was here to investigate, selecting their target before he even arrived on Vesa. If that were so, it would imply an even larger organization than anyone suspected, one with Galaxy-wide connections. Such scouts would perhaps try to chase away anyone who got involved with their target, since it would add a complication to their plans—as well as someone who might raise a hue and cry if the victim turned up missing.

That solution was farfetched, but possible. Yvette wondered at the logistics, though. After all, the expense of sending out teams of scouts to line up targets in that way would not be a paying venture. So many rich people visited Vesa anyhow that it would seem much more feasible to pick and choose among potential victims once they were on-planet.

What seemed more likely to her was that she happened to stumble into the middle of a situation that was independent of the Vesa problem. Those three blasterbats had not really been interested in her at all, but merely in the fact that she was becoming involved with Dak Lehman. They had not started following her until after she'd begun dating Dak, and even then they'd taken no active role until they'd established that something might come of the relationship. And at that, their warning to her had been extremely gentle, all things considered. They could just as easily have killed her, she knew. And they wanted her to know that.

She spent a good deal of that night wondering how to respond to the warning. Her d'Alembert pride had been injured, and that clan was known as particularly stiff-necked. She did not like being threatened, and she did not like appearing as though she were giving in. Yvette had a strong contempt for weak-willed women who pretended to be at the mercy of big, strong men; she was living proof of equality between the sexes and hated having to subordinate herself.

Dak was obviously in some kind of trouble. Three expert men wouldn't suddenly start following him around just for the hell of it. Dak himself seemed to know something; Yvette recalled all the times when he'd started to tell her something, only to shy away and go silent at the last moment. What could be the matter with this seemingly ideal man? She cared a great deal about him, and was caring more every day; she couldn't just stand by while he was in danger and not make a move to help him.

But yet, she had a job of her own to do. Dak's problem could very well be independent of hers—and if that were the case, it would be unwise of her to get mixed up in it. Fighting on two fronts at once was not terribly smart, if it could be avoided.

Finally she just decided to take a wait-and-see attitude. She would not seek out Dak and his problems—but if he should come to her, she would not avoid them. The d'Alembert family did not believe in dodging responsibility.

After the usual hectic debarking procedures and a short wait going through customs, Yvette had her luggage sent to the Hotel Regulus where she had booked her reservations in advance. The Regulus was one of the hundreds of plush hotels on Vesa that specialized in catering to rich tourists visiting this gambler's paradise, and they knew how to treat a guest well—particularly one as wealthy as Carmen Velasquez. In no time at all, after crossing a number of palms with ten-ruble tips, Yvette found herself installed in her twelfth level suite. Looking around at the large group of rooms, including a living room, bedroom with imperial-sized bed, and spacious bathroom, she felt the slightest tinge of a letdown. *Traveling on a first-class liner like the* Empress Irene *must have really spoiled me,* she mused.

She was here to work, though, not luxuriate, and she'd better set about it. Enough time had already been wasted on the trip here. For all she knew, her brother might have wrapped up the case already.

The first thing she did was phone down to the desk and ask them to send up a newsroll. It arrived while she was still unpacking, and she sat down to read it at once. She glanced avidly through the personal ads, but there was nothing there yet. If Jules had wanted to contact her, he would have placed an ad signed "Frenchie." No such ad existed, which meant that he had not yet reached any conclusions strong enough to tell her about—either that or he was in no condition to place any ads in the paper. She dismissed that thought from her mind almost the instant it came up. Jules could take care of himself.

As soon as she'd finished her unpacking chores, Yvette decided to go out and immediately taste some of the pleasures that Vesa had to offer. The stack of guidebooks she had brought along told her of some of the better casinos in the area near her hotel, and she checked off three that interested her the most. Then she changed her clothes preparatory to making her debut in Vesan society.

Her basic outfit was a jumpsuit made from a patterned brocade fabric of deep rose and gold. Gold boots covered her feet and a belt of gold squares set with pearls circled her waist, holding up a red velvet purse. The turtleneck collar of her jumpsuit was also lavishly adorned with pearls. Her dark brown hair was swept up and crowned by a coronet braid of red velvet dotted with pearls.

Over the jumpsuit she wore a ruby-red velvet houppelande, with dagged sleeves that reached to the ground and a high collar that came up well past her ears. The houppelande was fastened at the throat with an enormous golden pin, in the center of which reposed a fist-sized ruby. A golden string of matched pearls—each the size of a walnut—draped loosely around her neck.

Yvette eyed herself critically in the mirror. *It screams rich,* she told herself. *Rich, but tasteful.* Ready at last, she left her rooms to face the rigors of Vesa.

It didn't take her long to realize that Vesa was a strange place. She had known intellectually that all life on this moon existed in underground caverns carved from the naked rock; but knowing that fact and actually experiencing it were two different things. The subterranean aspects could be ignored when one was inside a building; after all, people are used to having ceilings over their heads when they're in a room.

What was not so usual was to have a roof over you when you were "outside." The broad transportation corridors, with their constant streams of busy traffic flowing by, were exactly like streets on any civilized world in the Galaxy, except for the fact that there was a ceiling of solid stone overhead. This was not so bad at the major intersections, where the ceiling was a dome that rose perhaps fifteen or twenty meters over the ground level; but in the tunnels that linked the major caverns, the roof would come down to less than a meter in spots over the tops of the vehicles traversing the roads. It was a situation that could produce claustrophobia in even the stoutest of hearts, and Yvette found that, for the first couple of days, she had to fight down the incipient fear that the ceiling would cave in on her head at any moment.

Adding to the underground nature of the environment was the fact that Vesa was a maze that sometimes defied the best analytical minds. A labyrinth of tunnels, some of them running for kilometers in length, connected a series of large and small caverns in a seemingly random pattern that only longtime residents were able to decipher. Yvette became lost almost the instant she drove away from her hotel in one of the ubiquitous jits that served as Vesa's mass transportation system. The driver had never heard of the casino she wanted to visit, and so he took her to another. "They're all pretty much the same," was his philosophical comment. "You can lose your money just as fast at one as at another." She never did find the one she had originally set out for.

After two days of traveling around, though, she came to the conclusion that the driver had been wrong. True, to the casual eye all the casinos did look alike—flashy rooms filled with flashy people, bright lights glaring from all directions, loud music pumped through the atmosphere intermingling with the brash spiels of barkers trying to lure people to this or that area that was less crowded at the moment. The smells of incense, dopesticks, cigarettes and a thousand and one individual perfumes assaulted the nostrils. Several times Yvette found herself feeling terribly nostalgic, for the flavor was almost like that of the midway of her beloved Circus—though the midway had always been far less frantic and far more innocent.

The more careful observer, though, could see slight differences between the different gambling spots. Some of them were cheaper, appealing to the tourists with only moderate amounts of money to squander, while others were ultraposh and almost flaunted their exclusivity. Some places tended to be the preserve of older married couples, while others were definitely the hangout of young singles out for a good time. Some casinos were brash and garish while others were—for Vesa—almost reserved and dignified. Each casino had a character and clientele uniquely its own. But no matter where she went, from the plushest clubs to the lowest dives, there were crowds. Hundred upon thousands of people jammed into spaces that would have been cramped with half that many present. Gambling fever was almost a tangible commodity, a madness infecting everyone around her. It was as though people, having spent so much of their money just in getting here, felt a desperate desire to lose the rest of it at the gambling tables. Some of the more intense gamblers went without food or sleep for a day or more at a time.

The magnitude of her problem was beginning to hit home to her. In this faceless mass of human bodies, it was quite easy to see how thirty-five a day could disappear without anyone even noticing. They would be replaced as quickly as they vanished by equally faceless bodies awaiting the slaughter. Yvette had spent a goodly amount of time on Earth, one of the most highly populated planets in the Empire, and thought she had known what crowding was like, but this made humanity's mother planet look like the wide open spaces. The effect of these surging masses was to dehumanize everyone involved—a result that left Yvette terribly depressed, despite the showy glamor of the moon.

It took her only the initial two days of exploration to establish a pattern for herself. In keeping with the character of Carmen Velasquez, she narrowed her field down to a handful of casinos that catered to the younger, richer, hipper crowd. The general age level of the customers at these places was under forty; the clothing was all sharp and in accordance to the latest fashions from the various sectors of the Empire. Dopesticks were more common in this crowd than either cigarettes or alcohol, though hardly *de rigeur*. The talk was a bit louder, the conversations more intense, the laughter more spontaneous and natural.

There was a certain repetition of clientele at these places, and after a couple of days of regular attendance Yvette learned most of the regulars by sight, and a couple by name. She struck up casual conversations with them and managed to get her story across. It was impossible to tell who might be an agent of the conspiracy, so Yvette was ready to talk to anyone who showed even a casual interest in her.

Her gambling habits were quite simple—she stuck to card games exclusively. Her father and uncle were both masters at cards and she had sat in on many a hand late at night after the Circus had closed to the rubes, absorbing their knowledge and tricks. She knew any number of methods of cheating, but did not try them here; the house dealers were too sharp and Carmen Velasquez was not supposed to be a professional. She did, however, manage to come out a good distance ahead in the long run, and quickly earned a joking reputation among her newfound friends as a cardsharp.

"Where'd you ever learn to play like that?" one guy asked after she'd cleaned out his pockets one afternoon two weeks later.

"It sure as hell wasn't on Purity," said another fellow who had managed to retain at least some of his chips.

Yvette allowed herself a demure blush. "After my late husband and I made our fortune and got ourselves kicked off Purity for being too concerned with matters temporal instead of spiritual, we resolved to learn all about the pleasant vices. Gambling was Carlos' particular passion and he kept insisting that I play cards with him. Unfortunately I was always better than he was, and it infuriated him when I won. He swore off gambling once for three whole weeks, he was so mad. I could take it or leave it alone, which only made him feel worse. I suppose. . . ."

"Carmen!" The call of a familiar voice rang out across the room, and Yvette looked up, a curious mixture of emotions churning through her system.

Card games usually took place in side rooms off the main gambling hall. These rooms were smaller and a bit less cramped, since most of the tourists preferred to lose their money quickly and impersonally at the machines and gaming tables. Cards were a comparatively slow and more involved method of gambling, and appealed only to a minority of the crowd.

Across this smaller room, hazy though it was with smoke, Yvette could see Dak Lehman making his way through the press of people towards her table. He must have spotted her from the doorway, she reasoned. The expression on his face as he came over to her was a combination of delight and concern.

"I thought for a while I'd never find you," he said as he finally reached her side. "I've been looking everywhere for you ever since we landed here. I was almost beginning to give up hope. It was as if Vesa had just swallowed you up or something."

Yvette cast him a startled glance. *Does he know something about the disappearances?* she wondered, scrutinizing his expression carefully. But no, there was nothing menacing or secretive there. It had obviously been a chance remark that meant more to her than it did to him. Recovering, she said offhandedly, "This is just such an incredible place it's easy to get lost. I'm sorry you had to go through such a hassle to find me."

"The only thing that matters is that I *have* found you," Dak replied earnestly. Then, looking around at the other people seated at Yvette's table, he continued in a lower voice, "Can we go somewhere to talk privately?"

"I don't really think there's anyplace private on this entire moon," Yvette said, standing up and sweeping her winnings into her purse with one confident motion. "It's all so crowded I sometimes feel selfish when I shower by myself. But if we walk around the casino I don't think anyone'll overhear what we say."

Dak took her arm and escorted her out into the main casino area. The din out here was so loud that they practically had to shout in each other's ear to make themselves understood, but Yvette was right—the nearest thing to private was being in the middle of a noisy, uncaring crowd.

"You left me last time with an unanswered question between us," he said. "You told me you'd think about it, and that was several weeks ago. Have you come to any conclusions,"

Yvette looked away from him and took a long deep sigh before answering. "I don't want you to think I've been avoiding you these past weeks, because I haven't. I just haven't had the time to go actively looking for you."

"That's an evasion, not an answer."

"I know. I can't give you the answer you want, I'm afraid. I find you a most attractive man, Dak, and there are more odd moments than I'd care to mention when I have to snap myself out of a daydream about what it would be like married to you. But I just can't convince myself it would work. Putting aside all the romantic clichés about love conquering all, there are too many barriers in our way."

She explained about the physical problems stemming from their different planetary backgrounds, problems that would lead to either him being a cripple or her an exile. She could not, of course, tell him the real story about her family and her job; instead, she leaned heavily on her love for her dear departed Carlos and how she could not bring herself to "betray" him so soon after his death.

Dak's expression was grim as he listened to her speak, but he did not interrupt even once. She tried to finish with as soft a cushion as she could. "I love you, I really do. That goodnight kiss you gave me last time had me floating through the air on my way back to my suite, even in one gee. I'm not just saying this to make you feel better; it's the way I feel. But for all the reasons I've told you, plus a few personal ones, I don't think we could sustain a long-term relationship. We'll both be much better off if we break apart now, before our emotions get totally out of hand."

Dak scowled, and an angry gleam appeared in his eyes. He was not apparently used to being turned down in something he wanted. "I still love you, Carmen," he said evenly. "Being apart from you these past few weeks has made my longing stronger, not weaker. You say you love me, too. But your reasons for not wanting to marry me just don't hold air. We can overcome any problems we set our minds to. We both have a good deal of money, we can go back and forth between a heavy gravity world and a lighter one. I can buy machines to help me withstand your stronger gravity. I . . ."

His voice had been rising with each sentence, until it took on an almost hysterical tone. She raised a hand to silence him. "Dak, please, this is getting us nowhere."

He stopped, caught his breath, and then continued in a more reasonable tone, "Look I've been invited to a really swank party tonight. It's being given by one of the big shots on Vesa, a man named Garst. Why don't you come along with me and we can talk about this some more then? I'd be delighted to have your company, and. . . ."

"I don't think I'm getting through to you. It will not work between us, and all the talking you do will not make it work. No, I won't go with you tonight; there would be no point to it."

The anger dropped suddenly out of Dak, and he looked instead like a frightened little boy. "Don't drop me forever," he begged. There was a hint of tears in his eyes. "I really don't think I could take that, Carmen; you've become too special to me. Please—if you won't come to the party then at least say you'll meet me tomorrow and we can visit some casinos together."

There was such an air of desperation to his voice that Yvette had to relent. She did love him, and it tore her up inside to see him so affected. "All right," she said softly, "I'll meet you tomorrow, but only for a little while. I have things to do myself, you know. Where and when do you want to meet?"

"Right here at, say, eleven hundred." Dak's face had brightened perceptibly at her sudden capitulation.

"All right," Yvette nodded. "But I have to be going for now; there are things I must do." She stood on her toes to reach up and kiss him, intending to give him only a slight peck. But suddenly his arms were around her and the simple kiss was turning into far more passionate a thing than she had planned.

When finally they did part, she was feeling a little wobbly on her feet. "Whew. See you tomorrow," she said as she started to walk off.

"Don't be late," he called after her. As an afterthought, he added, "If you should need to get in touch with me for any reason, I'm staying at the Soyuz Hotel."

Yvette just barely heard him, for her keen senses were trained elsewhere at the moment. She had picked up a tail again—Murgatroyd. Apparently even this chance run-in with Dak had been enough to set off the curiosity of that band that was so interested in Gospodin Lehman's welfare.

Yvette did not go straight back to her hotel as she'd intended. She had no way of knowing whether the trio who had ambushed her knew where she was staying on Vesa—but if they didn't know, she certainly didn't want to show them. In a concerted effort to lose her tail, Yvette went through the main halls of the three most crowded casinos she knew, changed jits repeatedly as she drove all over the tourist district of Vesa, and ducked into a ladies' room for over an hour before emerging with her houppelande over her arm to give her an entirely different appearance. There was no sign of Murgatroyd following her by this time so, realizing that she couldn't just keep

73

wandering the moon all night, she decided to risk going back to her room.

Once inside, she bolted the door and pulled up a chair to sit facing it, just in case the shadows were to try another attack. She kept herself awake until early in the morning.

CHAPTER 7

A Meeting at the Warehouse

As he stared at the men from Chandakha, Jules realized that he was the only other person in the crew who had witnessed their deliberate murder of Rask. Everyone else was coming from the other side of the spacefield, and the body of the scraper machine had been interposed between them and the Chandakhari. As the rest of the group, led by Fizcono, now pulled up to the scene, all they would see was the dead body of their former comrade lying at the feet of the coterie of Chandakhari.

Jules thought quickly. He was the only one who knew the Chandakhari had murdered Rask with deliberate efficiency. But if they thought he knew that, he might become their next target. All in all, he decided to feign ignorance of exactly what happened. They must know he had seen them do it, but by pretending not to know he could plant some doubt in their minds.

So, just as Fizcono and the rest of the crew came around the corner of the scraper, he asked, "What happened to him?"

Forakhi, the unofficial leader of the Chandakhari group, locked his gaze with that of Jules, as though trying to read the SOTE agent's soul. "We tried to hold him, but he was like a madman," Forakhi said slowly, his eyes never wavering. "We backed him up against the scraper, but he was squirming so much that he tore his suit on it." He was defying Jules to contradict him; Jules said nothing.

74

Fizcono knelt beside Rask's body and verified for himself that the man was dead. "More drapping reports to fill out!" he muttered savagely under his breath. Then, standing up and looking at the Chandakhari for a long moment, he said aloud, "I guess you men did the best you could, under the circumstances. You'll all have to write up your versions of what happened, of course; insurance companies are fussy about that sort of thing."

Then he turned specifically to Jules. "Nice work, duChamps. I can't recall ever seeing anyone move so fast and so well. Where did you learn all that, anyhow?"

"I was on the gymnastics team in school," Jules lied smoothly. "Guess I've always kept myself pretty much in shape."

Fizcono accepted that story with a grunt and began issuing orders to have Rask's body taken back inside to the infirmary. The rest of the men he told to go back to work, though even he did not expect them to be able to accomplish much—not after the work day had started like this. Still, they were getting paid to do a job and it was his responsibility to see that they did it. He resigned himself to having his crew fall even farther behind in their work than they already were, and followed Rask's body back inside to answer the questions he knew the front office would ask.

To no one's surprise, the work that day went very lackadaisically. They loaded less than half of what they should have onto a departing freighter, much to the chagrin of the captain who bawled them out over the radio for dawdling when he had a schedule to keep. The men ignored his rantings and went on at their own speed, still stunned by what happened earlier.

Every so often, Jules would look up from his job to see one of the Chandakhari—notably Radapur or Forakhi —staring at him, as though trying to figure out what sort of a game he was playing. Jules pretended not to notice their attention and kept on with his work.

When the shift was finally over and everyone was unsuiting back in the locker room, Jules was surprised when Radapur, the young Chandakhar, actually came over to talk to him. "You saved my life out there," the lad said.

"Rask was going to kill me, and you were the only one who acted quickly enough to stop him."

"Somebody had to," Jules shrugged. Open displays of gratitude embarrassed him, and he hoped Radapur would not be too flowery about it.

"Nevertheless, it was you who did it." The youth held out his hand and Jules shook it vigorously. "I won't forget what you did for me. Maybe someday I'll have the chance to do a favor for you."

Jules was about to reply that such a thing was not necessary and that he would have done the same for anyone, but he didn't get the chance. Forakhi, with a whistle and a sharp look, called Radapur back to the Chandakhari group. As Jules watched, Forakhi spoke a few sharp words in the youth's ear, obviously admonishing him not to speak with anyone from outside their little clique. The lad cast one long look back over his shoulder at Jules, then returned to his group.

Everyone who was involved in the scuffle had to stay a little late in order to tape-record their versions of the story for the administration personnel. Forakhi and the rest of the Chandakhari were visibly chafing at this delay, as though they had some appointment to go to and were being kept from it. At last everyone was released and told to go home; but instead of following that advice, Jules chose to follow the Chandakhari instead.

They left the port building as a group and flagged down one of the roving jits. Jules cursed the haphazard transportation system of Vesa under his breath; he didn't want to let his quarries get away from him that simply. Fortunately, he was able to commandeer a jit directly behind theirs and, using the excuse that he and his friends had gotten separated and he didn't have the address of where they were supposed to be going, he convinced the driver to follow the other jit. The large tip he handed the man probably did not hurt his cause, either.

They drove through a confusing maze of tunnels, changing direction so many times that Jules began to get worried that they knew he was following them. But they made no attempt to speed up or lose him on sharp turns, so he relaxed and guessed that they were only taking a precautionary route to their destination.

Finally the other jit stopped and the Chandakhari got out. Jules' driver had done such a good job of staying with them that he arrived almost right behind them, and Jules had to dawdle about getting out of the jit for fear that his quarries would spot him.

Actually, despite the long and complicated route they had taken, the Chandakhari had ended up at a point not too far distant from where they'd started. They were in the warehouse district where the goods unloaded from the incoming ships were stored before being distributed to the rest of Vesa. Jules emerged from his jit as the group he was following entered the front door of one warehouse.

Jules looked quickly around for another way into the building. He couldn't go in the same way the Chandakhari had, or he'd be spotted for sure. His sharp eyes instantly detected what he was looking for—a freight elevator tube beside the building. Structures on Vesa were built down rather than up, into the bedrock of the moon for sturdier support. Jules did not want to activate the elevator itself, for it might make some noise that would alarm the group he was pursuing; but the tube did have a series of hand-holds along its length for the use of repair crews, and Jules descended this ladder until he came to a service door in the wall. The door was locked, and he had to stand on a small ledge for two minutes experimenting with the various master keys he always carried with him before he could get it to open.

He found himself on the third level of the warehouse. The large room was dimly-lit and filled with row upon row of the large airtight crates that he was becoming all too familiar with. Apparently this was a section for storing goods that had not yet been unpacked.

Jules strained his ears, but could hear no sounds around him. Moving with a silence that would put a cat to shame, he eased his way into the warehouse, using the large containers as cover while he explored the aisles at this level. No one was here.

Now there was a choice to make. Should be go upward in search of his group and check out the top two levels, or should he go even further down? He decided down would be best; a group of conspirators would want to be as far from the front door as possible, to avoid being overheard by casual passersby.

Gently sloping ramps led from level to level, broad corridors for lift trucks and dollies to carry their loads. The ramps were possible points of exposure, since there was no place for him to hide on them, but short of chancing the elevator tube again they were his only method of getting from one level to the next. Stealthily he crept downward to the fourth level, only to find it, too, deserted. On the fifth level, however, he struck paydirt.

He could hear the low muttering of voices when he was halfway down the ramp, and he slowed his pace at once. Hugging tightly to the wall he slithered down to the floor level and behind the protective cover of some half-opened crates. From here, he was able to pick his way slowly forward until he had a clear view of the entire scene.

The lighting on this level was as dim as throughout the rest of the warehouse, but Jules' eyes were by this time accustomed to the weak light. A large space had been cleared throughout the center of the floor, and along one semicircular section of the area sat a group of perhaps thirty men. The first thing Jules noticed was that they all seemed to be Chandakhari; all of them had the swarthy complexion and straight black hair that marked the racial type, although some of the men were old enough that their hair was predominantly gray. Jules was startled to see men in their fifties and possibly even sixties sitting in that group, though the majority of the people were late thirties to early forties. Radapur, the lad from Jules' work crew, was the youngest one there.

Before this group, like a teacher in front of a class, was a tall, thin, well-dressed man with a narrow face and harsh eyes. He sat at ease with his legs dangling casually over the edges of a pair of packing boxes placed end to end for his convenience. He had a clipboard on his lap and he was reading casually from it: ". . . Group Three, weekly intake of five thousand, seven hundred and sixty-two rubles, which means Group Two's area seems to be the richest at the moment. I think we'll leave Three where it is for now and move in One to back Two up. Group Four, I don't have your numbers yet; where are they?"

A man at one side of the semicircle spoke up. "Pakkan was delayed at the last moment; he'll try to be here shortly."

The man in front grimaced. "This has been a bad week for obstacles and delays. All the other sectors may get ahead of us." He stared directly at the group of Jules' coworkers. "Your little unofficial forays have been noted and will count against you. You have repeatedly been told that we act for money only, not vengeance. We must not allow ourselves to get personally involved in our calling. Any emotion, even vengeance, will lead eventually to a weakening of will and infirmity of purpose. We must keep our minds and souls pure if we are to succeed.

"Back to business. I can't make final assignments for the week until I hear how Group Four has done, but assuming they have maintained their average I think I can tentatively shift them over to pick up the area being vacated by One. Group One then will operate near Two— say, around the Lucky Streak Casino. Two and Three will stay as they are for now. . . ."

Jules heard footsteps coming down the ramp behind him. This would probably be the member of Group Four who was late—and if so, Jules' position would be exposed. He looked quickly around for a spot that could not be seen from either the back or the front and, the instant he spotted it, he dove in that direction.

But his motion was far too late. The tardy murderer was at the point on the ramp where he could just see into the fifth level, and Jules' rapid movement attracted his attention. For a second he froze, then realized that his mates had not known they were being spied upon. "Hey, there's somebody else in here!" he called out.

The other Chandakhari jumped to attention at his cry. They were paranoid about outsiders anyway, and this alarm set off their worst fears. Several of the men had been wearing small jeweled daggers at their belts, and their hands went automatically to their waists to remove the weapons. All of them looked around to see if they could spot the intruder, but Jules' chosen spot did provide him with a maximum amount of coverage.

The newcomer, who saw where Jules had gone, noted the confusion of his fellows. "Down there!" he pointed. "Behind those boxes!"

All stealth was useless now, Jules knew. He was up against better than thirty men who knew precisely where he was. Speed, strength and agility were the tools he would have to use if he wanted to survive beyond the next few minutes. Bracing his back against a row of heavy crates, he lifted his legs and kicked out at the series of boxes stacked in front of him. Two of the stacks teetered ominously for a moment; then, as he gave them a second kick, they toppled over onto the crowd of men that had started after him.

The effects of Vesa's gravity made the spectacle almost ludicrous, as the boxes fell in slow motion towards their targets and the men strained to get out of the path of the falling objects. Finally, after what seemed like ages, the boxes hit the floor and shattered, scattering their contents—small metal machine parts—all over the floor and making the footing treacherous.

But Jules had not stayed put to watch the results of his action. Survival depended on movement, and Jules was a veritable blur. The low gravity both hampered and helped; hampered because it took so long for objects to reach ground once they were in the air, and helped because his reflexes, attuned to gravitational pulls twelve times as strong, were like lightning compared to those of his adversaries. In fact, he had to be constantly adjusting his strengths downward, or he would have ended up overshooting each goal.

A knife flew by his head, but not too close. So slowly was it going that he could have snatched it out of mid-air and thrown it back at its owner had he desired. Instead, he let it continue along its flight path and bury itself two centimeters deep into a wood crate. He was not too worried about the knives these murderers were carrying; he had given them a good scan and realized that they were not properly balanced for throwing. Jules' cousin, Jean d'Alembert, was an expert knife thrower, and Jules knew most of the fundamentals of that art just from observing a professional in action. The blades in evidence here were all intended for stabbing; if Jules let any of these men get that close to him the game would be up anyhow—and he knew it.

Jules quickly ducked down a cross row of crates, hoping to win access to the ramp and freedom. His way was blocked, though, by half a dozen of the crooks advancing on him with murder in their eyes. Gauging the distances, Jules decided against trying to leap over their heads; a strategic retreat would be a better tactic right here. With a quick turn, he fled back in the direction from which he'd come.

Two thugs leaped at him from atop a packing crate on his right. One of them gripped Jules' wrist while the other tried to get hold of the SOTE agent's waist. With the sheer force of his strength, Jules whipped his right hand around, pulling the attached attacker with it and banging the man's head solidly against a steel container. With a dull groan that was barely audible over the clang of the collision, the man released his grip on Jules' hand and fell unconscious to the floor.

With an athlete's disdain for wasted motion, Jules continued with the follow-through on his toss. His body spun around counterclockwise, and the crook who had been grasping for his waist slipped away and started falling to the floor. Jules did not allow that fall to continue unassisted, though; as he spun, he jerked his left foot backwards and clipped the murderer under the chin with his heel. The man was out cold before touching ground.

Leaping nimbly over his two fallen foes, Jules continued along his chosen path, even though each step took him that much further away from the ramp. Over to his left, a group of four men were cutting diagonally across the floor in an attempt to intercept his path. Running at top speed, Jules deliberately rammed his body into another stack of boxes, which fell slowly but hard into the middle of that group. The men had all been running too fast to be able to stop and dodge. Most of them were able to lift up their arms to fend off the falling boxes, but the sharp edge of one container caught one of the Chandakhari squarely across the top of his head, cutting open a large gash. The man fell to the floor under the weight of the box, blood oozing slowly from the cut.

His intentional collision with the stack of boxes had also affected Jules' balance. He staggered a bit from the impact and was just about to recover when his foot slipped on one of the metal pieces from the first stack of boxes he'd knocked over. Trying desperately to recover his balance, he stumbled into another stack of boxes and got the wind knocked out of his lungs. He had to stand still for a second to recover from the blow.

As he stood there for a moment, three more of the thugs came charging at him. He was able to sidestep one completely, and the man went running right past him into the same stack of crates Jules had just hit. The second man received a karate chop down on the back of his neck, and it snapped his spine; Jules was fighting for his life, now, and had no time to pull his punches. When he hit, it was with the full power of an angry DesPlainian.

The third man just happened to tackle Jules' bad left leg, sending a stab of pain through the agent's body. The two men fell hard to the floor, but Jules quickly recovered from the initial shock of the encounter. Bringing up his right knee, he clipped his assailant under the chin and the man fell backwards. Jules rolled over and got quickly to his feet again, ready for more action.

Although he had significantly reduced his opposition, he was still vastly outnumbered. Now that the initial surprise of his presence was wearing off, these Chandakhari were beginning to react as fighting units once more. Jules had had one taste already of how efficient they could be; he had no desire for further demonstrations. They were traveling in packs now, circling in slowly and hoping to get the chance to use their special techniques on him. He had to keep away from them as much as possible, for each second they slowed him down gave the mob that much more time to close in. He would never be able to escape from twenty determined stranglers if they all got their hands on him at once.

The killers were coming toward him from three sides now—from the direction of the ramp and the direction exactly opposite it, and from the front where the group had been seated. That left him only the back wall to retreat to—a move which the enemy obviously expected. Not wishing to disappoint them, Jules made his way through the aisles of boxes to the back wall, then turned to face the attackers.

They were moving toward him a bit more slowly now, confident of the final outcome and not wanting to spoil things by tipping their hand too quickly. Overreaction could be disastrous; they had their quarry boxed in and could afford to take the time to do it right.

Jules faced slightly to his right, away from the direction of the ramp, and seemed to be giving that third of his attackers the majority of his attention. With his peripheral vision, however, he was keeping close tabs on the advancement of the group in front of him and to the left. Suddenly, when the positions were exactly right, he made his move.

From a standing start, he began running straight at the group coming from his left. They were a bit startled at this direct assault, but they held their line firm and prepared to meet the onslaught. Jules built up as much speed as he could and, when he came within five meters of the killers, suddenly bent his legs under him and leaped through the air in a low arc over the heads of the startled group. One of the killers, a bit faster on the uptake than the rest, tried to jump up as Jules passed overhead and grab some part of his clothing to at least slow him up; all he received for his efforts, though, was a kick in the face as Jules used his aerialist's skills to twist about in midleap. The jumper fell violently back into the midst of his fellows, creating more pandemonium.

The powerful muscles of Jules' legs acted as springs when he landed again, absorbing much of the shock of impact. He rolled over forward once to absorb most of the rest of the momentum, then, in one continuous motion, sprang to his feet and began running toward the ramp. There was no one to block his way now, no obstacles to overcome; Jules could concentrate purely on speed.

And speed he did. On DesPlaines, Jules in his best form would have been considered a fast runner, though perhaps not a record holder. The recent injury to his leg slowed him down more. But on worlds with lower gravities, there was just no comparison. Jules was far and away the fastest man these crooks ever had or ever would see, a blur in human form. He had reached the ramp before any of the Chandakhari could even think to pursue him in that direction.

They did try to give chase, of course. To a man they raced in the direction of the ramp and upward to the next level. But Jules had had too much of a jump on them and was moving far too fast, tired though he was from all the fighting. By the time the first ones reached the fourth level, the only trace left of Jules d'Alembert was the sound of his receding footsteps as he raced upward and out of the building.

Garst was not pleased. Lessin, the man who had been conducting the briefing in the warehouse before the interruption occurred, had gone straight to his boss with the news of the intruder. Now he was not so sure it was the safest thing he could have done.

"To be spied on is one thing, but to have discovered the spy and let him get away is rank incompetence!" Garst's short, corpulent body was trembling with rage. Lessin knew those rages—in fact, had seen them directed at other people. The results were never pleasant, and he mentally braced himself for the punishment he knew would come.

"We all tried," he began to apologize. "I've never seen a man move like that before. He was like a wild animal. . . ."

"And you only outnumbered him thirty-three to one," Garst sneered. "Panna-cats have been caught barehanded at smaller odds than those. Your men are all well-trained and good at their jobs; most of them have been with us for years, yet you could not catch one simple person." He banged his palm with his fist in frustration.

Lessin waited in silence for Garst's rage to blow over. Anything he could say would only add to the fury the other felt.

At length, Garst's temper subsided a little. He turned his back on Lessin and walked around behind his large desk. "The question now is, who was that man? What kind of threat does he represent? Was he acting on his own, or are there others with him?"

"The men from my Group Two know him. He started working at the docks with them a couple of days ago. He calls himself Georges duChamps and he's originally from DesPlaines. They had a bit of a problem with other workers in their outfit and this duChamps intervened a couple of times—both for and against them. They can't figure him out."

"A DesPlainian, eh?" Garst settled himself behind his desk and drummed his fingers impatiently across the top. "Well, that may excuse *some* of your bungling; I've heard some pretty impressive things about them. But still—thirty-three to one. . . ." His voice trailed off and he shot Lessin a meaningful glance.

The subordinate decided to leap into the conversational breach before Garst had much chance to contemplate further on the mishap. "I think he was just working on his own. He'd had a few brush-ups with my men, and was curious about them, that's all. After all, he couldn't be with the police—they wouldn't dare interfere with us. . . ."

"But we can't be sure!" Garst banged a fist down hard on the solid wood desktop. "In this business, Lessin, we can't afford to take any chances at all. Take nothing for granted. There are other constabularies than our own, you know. So far, I grant you, they have not seen fit to intercede in our business, because we've been careful not to be too greedy. A little trickle diverted from a wide stream is never missed. But there is always the possibility that we slipped up somewhere and alerted someone. We must take great pains to find out the truth and, if that is the case, to rectify our error as quickly as possible."

Garst stood up once more and came around the desk to face his minion. "We must capture this duChamps fellow—alive. We have to question him to find out how much is known about us, so that we can assess the danger. If he is just a man on his own, well and good; he can be eliminated with no one being any the wiser. But if he is part of a larger force, more drastic measures will have to be taken. I hate to even think about that, but I know I'll have to."

He glowered sternly at Lessin. "Since it was you who bungled this matter, I'll let you be the one to straighten it up. You will direct the search operations. I want every single man we've got to have a description of duChamps. I want every single hiding place searched beginning, of course, with his hotel room, though I doubt he'd be fool enough to return there. We'll scour every centimeter of Vesa if we have to, but I want that duChamps found and brought to me alive. Is that understood?"

It was indeed understood. Lessin was actually glad Garst had put him in charge of the search. It had been duChamps' fault that he'd had to come to Garst with this problem in the first place, and he had that debt of honor to pay off. He would find the DesPlainian, all right—and when he was finished, the spy would wish Garst had allowed Lessin to kill him right away.

CHAPTER 8

Vanished!

Yvette got only about three hours' sleep following her chance meeting with Dak Lehman, and even that was spent fitfully sitting up in a chair, facing the door and starting at the slightest noise in the hall that might herald the return of the three men who had ambushed her on the starliner. They had caught her by surprise once, and she vowed that would never happen again. But this night was a false alarm; nothing untoward occurred.

At 0930 she finally dragged herself out of the chair to get ready for her rendezvous with Dak. She had neglected to wipe off the makeup from last night and it had gone gritty on her face. Added to that were the dark circles under her eyes and flyaway hair from sleeping in an awkward position. Taking a good look at herself in a mirror, she said, "Dak must be crazy; nobody in his right mind would ever want to marry someone who looks like that."

She gave serious consideration to calling him at his hotel and breaking off the date, or even just standing him up without telling him anything. She hadn't told him where she was staying; he might never be able to find her again, and all their mutual problems would be solved. But, with a sigh, she realized she could never do that. She had promised to meet him, and promises were sacred things to a d'Alembert. Her family pride would not permit her the luxury of breaking this one.

She spent an extra amount of care in making up her face this morning, and by the time she was finished much of the depression had left her. The face that stared back at her in the mirror was no longer haggard, and she declared herself satisfied with the results; a less modest person would have realized that she was devastatingly beautiful. A quick look at the clock beside her bed told her that she'd spent entirely too much time on her make-up, though—it was just past 1030. Dressing quickly, she hurried out to the elevator tube and up to the lobby level to grab a jit. There would be no breakfast for her this morning, though perhaps Dak and she could go for lunch somewhere.

She arrived at the appointed spot five minutes late, cursing her own tardiness and the complexity of Vesa's traffic. Yvette hated to be late for anything; it made her feel vaguely incompetent. She dashed out of her jit and into the crowded casino, where she began her search for Dak.

She did not see him immediately, and began to pray that he would be late, too, so that he wouldn't notice her own tardiness. Even at this hour, though, the casino was quite crowded; Vesa, being an underground settlement, did not depend on the arbitrary rhythms of daylight and darkness, and was in bloom around the clock. Dak might have been here, saw that she wasn't here, and decided to mingle in the mob for a few minutes until she showed up.

Yvette waited. One minute turned into five, then ten. Still there was no sign of Dak. Impatience began to play on her nerves, taking the form alternatively of anger and concern. *How dare he keep me waiting? He was the one who wanted this meeting so badly. But what if he's hurt? What if he slipped in his bathtub and got a concussion?*

She began to feel very conspicuous standing there alone in the entranceway while people milled around her intent on their gambling. Finally deciding to take matters into her own hands, she walked over to a public telephone, inserted a twenty-kopek piece in the slot and called the Soyuz Hotel where Dak had told her he was staying. "Connect me with Gospodin Lehman's room, please," she said when the hotel operator answered.

There was a momentary silence at the other end, then the voice came back, "I'm sorry, Gospodin Lehman has left."

Yvette sighed with relief. "You mean he's on his way to an appointment."

"I wouldn't know, gospozha."

"Khorosho. Thank you." She rang off and went back to the casino to continue her waiting.

She waited for half an hour longer, growing increasingly puzzled with each passing second. She knew it shouldn't take him more than fifteen minutes to get from his hotel to here. What could be keeping him?

Could some other business have come up so pressing that he had to stand her up without notifying her? She was modest enough to think that a lot of other things could be more important to him than she was, but she remembered the pleading, desperate tone he had used yesterday while begging her to meet him. He had sincerely meant that, and it was hard to imagine anything coming between him and this so-desired date.

But he wasn't here, and his hotel said he had left. Could there have been a traffic accident along the way? She looked outside and as far into the traffic tunnels as she could; there seemed to be no impediments to the flow of vehicles approaching the high-domed intersection outside the casino. For the moment she ruled out accident. But what was there left to explain his absence? *Where was he?* He couldn't have just vanished without a trace. . . .

Suddenly, Yvette froze with horror. *"Mon Dieu!"* she exclaimed under her breath. "It can't be. It just can't!"

But her logical mind told her that it all too easily could. What exactly had the hotel operator meant by saying he'd left? Suddenly, nothing was more important in the Universe to Yvette than finding out the answer. Racing outside to the sidewalk, she flagged down a jit. "Soyuz Hotel," she told the driver breathlessly. The woman nodded and calculated the rate from here to there. Yvette stuffed a wad of bills into the driver's hand without even bothering to count them and went to the back of the jit to sit by herself and think.

She found, though, that thinking was a difficult process at the moment. Her normally crisp, clear mind was drifting hopelessly in a sea of confusion, circling the problem without ever stopping to focus on it. She did not want to face the issue, even though she knew she'd have to in the immediate future. Her body was numb with fear, normally an alien emotion to her. Fear for herself was almost an unknown quantity, but fear for someone she cared about was a chilling thing.

After seven eternities the jit pulled up in front of the Soyuz Hotel. Yvette prodded her shocked body into action. Running out of the jit and into the lobby, she raced up to the desk clerk on duty. "Do you have a Gospodin Lehman registered here?"

The man checked his records. "We did. He checked out last night."

"Gospodin *Dak* Lehman?"

"That's correct."

"What time last night?"

The clerk consulted his records once more. "About 0130 hours."

"Isn't that rather a strange time to be checking out?"

"Not on Vesa," the clerk shrugged. "Time is meaningless here."

"Did he leave any forwarding address?" Yvette asked, grasping at straws.

"Sorry, none."

The realization of what must have happened was worse than a physical kick in the stomach. This was not some meaningless statistic in a musty old police file; this was a flesh-and-blood man whom she happened to love very much. It couldn't be true.

In desperation she ran to a public phone in the lobby and invested a small fortune in twenty-kopek pieces. She learned from Empress Spaceways, the company that owned the *Empress Irene,* that Dak Lehman had cashed in his return ticket and no, he had not bought one for a different date. Calls to every other transportation company servicing Vesa brought only negative results—Dak Lehman had not booked passage with any of them.

Like hundreds of thousand of people before him, Dak Lehman had vanished from the surface of Vesa without a trace.

When the conclusion was at last inescapable, Yvette sat down on the seat in the phone booth, turned her face toward the wall and cried. *Damn it, it was supposed to be me, Dak, not you. I was the target. I could have fought them back. Why did they take you and not me?*

Her brain felt as though it would burst, and the wall she was facing held no answers for her. She sobbed uncontrollably for several minutes, letting the emotion wash over her. When her grief had been expended, she lifted her head and the tears stopped flowing. Once again she was the cold, calculating supersecret agent, dedicated to the Service of the Empire. But the icy fury lurking behind her eyes would give warning to all that she was no longer a lady to tangle with casually. Yvette d'Alembert was out for blood.

She had started out of the booth when something across the hotel lobby caught her attention. Ducking back inside, she peered out through the crack in the door opening and watched the tall man she'd called Gaspard walk up to the desk and start a conversation with the clerk. From the way the clerk was shaking his head, it was a cinch that Gaspard was asking much the same thing

Yvette had asked—and was getting much the same answer. Yvette hoped that the clerk wouldn't mention the woman who had asked these same questions just a short while ago.

Apparently he didn't; from her own conversation, Yvette recalled that the man volunteered no information if he could possibly avoid it. At any rate, Gaspard grimaced at the clerk's answers and walked abruptly away from the counter out of Yvette's viewing range. The SOTE operative gave him a fifteen-second count, then opened the door and stepped out of the booth.

Gaspard was nowhere to be seen, so she surmised that he had left through the front door. Without a moment's indecision she went after him. He and his friends were her only lead right now; they knew more about Dak than they were telling. Perhaps her initial hunch was correct, that they were advance men for the conspiracy. But then why had this tall one been so upset that Dak was no longer at his hotel?

At any rate, there were no other clues to follow. Even if her ambushing trio were not personally responsible for Dak's fate (she could not bring herself, even now, to think "death"), they had been following him around much more closely than she had. They must have seen something that could help her in her further search.

Besides, she had a debt to repay them . . . and a d'Alembert debts are always paid.

Gaspard got on a jit driving eastward through one of the tunnels. Yvette was able to flag down an empty jit whose driver was more than delighted to take Yvette's generous tip in return for following another shuttle. Yvette sat right behind her driver, her sharp eyes watching for any sign that her quarry was aware he was being followed, but the man was obviously too engrossed in his own thoughts for that.

The ride was short and straight, only half a kilometer to the next domed intersection. There Gaspard got off and went into a sidewalk cafe. He emerged a few seconds later with a cup of hot liquid and a small tray of food. Finding a table all to himself, he sat and slowly nibbled at his lunch, with apparent unconcern for the passing of time. Yvette, who had gotten off her jit and walked across the street from the cafe, watched his actions through the mirror of her compact while she pretended to be making up her face. She decided he must be waiting for someone, probably one or both of his partners.

Her guess was confirmed several minutes later when Murgatroyd joined him. By this time, Yvette had put away her compact and was observing the action across the street by watching the reflections in a shop window. The two men across the way did not say anything at first, and then began talking in low tones. As Gaspard explained his findings, Murgatroyd became slightly more agitated. By the time the third man—a nondescript fellow with gray-brown hair and a pencil-thin mustache—joined them, they were both pretty upset.

The newcomer scowled when he was told the story. Abruptly, all three men stood up and walked out of the cafe. To Yvette's great relief they did not take a jit—it was too damned awkward trying to follow those infernal things each time—but walked instead down the street to the entrance of a small, inexpensive hotel called the Vesa Arms. Yvette, across the street, followed them, then crossed back to their side as they went into the hotel. She waited outside the door for ten seconds, then followed them inside.

She came through the door just in time to see the three of them disappearing down an elevator tube, apparently going to one of the hotel's sleeping rooms. She had no way of knowing which level they were going to or what their room number was, but she knew how to find out.

Think slut, she told herself. Unfastening the front of her jumpsuit almost down to the waist and draping the houppelande casually over her shoulder, she sauntered over to the hotel desk with a suggestive swing to her hips. She was perhaps a little overdressed to be a common *dyevka*, but she doubted the clerk would pay much attention to that detail.

"You see them three guys that just walked through here?" she asked in as slangy an accent as she could muster.

"Yeah," the clerk responded. "What about 'em?"

"I gotta know their room number."

"Why?" The clerk's eyes narrowed suspiciously.

"It's business."

"What kind of business would you have with them?"

"Very personal business," Yvette winked. "If you know what I mean."

The clerk knew very well what she meant. "If they wanted you with them, how come they didn't take you themselves?"

Yvette winked again. "They, uh, didn't want to be seen with me in the lobby." Her voice took on a more desperate whine. "Look, *tovarishch,* you gotta help me out. Gospodin Ivanov and his two friends. . . ."

"His name's not Ivanov," the clerk said curtly.

"They're all Ivanov to me. Anyway, he and his two friends asked me down to his room for a little while, only they left and forgot to tell me the number. It's dumb, I know, but some guys are like that. They'll be really mad if I don't get down there soon, and if they learn that you wouldn't give me their room number. . . ." Her tone of voice implied that dire things might happen.

"Twenty rubles," the clerk said.

"You're crazy!" Yvette exclaimed. "I'm only gettin' a hundred myself. I ain't givin' no drappin' twenty percent commission to no drappin' hotel clerk! Ten roobs is *it!*" Actually, Yvette could have paid the twenty and considered it a bargain; but she had to stay believably in character, and the clerk might have been suspicious if she hadn't argued.

The man behind the desk paused, then nodded. "Smooth, ten. In advance." His palm snaked out toward her across the counter.

Muttering something about "drappin' blackmail," Yvette fished deep into her purse and pulled out a ten-ruble bill. The desk clerk accepted it with an oily grin and said, "Room 412. Have a good time."

"Go bite yourself," Yvette retorted as she swiveled her hips over to the down elevator tube. As she dropped on a cushion of air to the fourth level she did allow herself a tight little smile for an act well done. The professional in her was pleased with her performance, though the woman part had little to be happy about at the moment.

The hallway on the fourth level was narrow, but deserted. Dim overhead lighting did little to illuminate the faded red carpet underfoot or the paint that was peeling off the wall in large chunks. The dead smell of old dopesticks lingered through the corridor, causing Yvette's sensitive nostrils to wrinkle in disgust. Somehow, the place just seemed to fit the characters of the three men she was after.

Room 412 was down the hall to her left as she emerged from the tube. Sneaking silently up to it, she put her ear to the door and listened. The sound of three male voices in conversation was plain; though she couldn't make out too many individual words, the fact that they were arguing about something was readily apparent.

After placing her houppelande on the floor and backing off from the door as far as the narrow hallway would allow, Yvette charged the portal at top speed. She hit the door with the full strength of her seventy-kilogram Des-Plainian body and the door, made only of cheap rikwood, gave way. As it burst inward, Yvette d'Alembert blew like a whirlwind into the room.

The three men inside never had a chance. Gaspard and Murgatroyd were seated on the bed, while the third —who appeared to be their boss—sat on a chair facing them. Surprised as they were by Yvette's sudden entrance, they had no time to move before she was on top of them. Murgatroyd was dispatched immediately with a sharp blow at the base of his neck. Gaspard turned his head toward her just in time to get a knee jerked savagely into his face. As he doubled over with the pain, Yvette grabbed the back of his shirt and used it to fling him against the wall, where he hit his head and slumped to the floor, unconscious.

The third man had a moment to rise from his chair and reach into his jacket, fishing for a gun. Yvette was over to him in a flash, grabbed his wrist before he could withdraw his weapon and smashed it down hard against her knee. The man howled with pain as his wrist bone cracked, but Yvette's store of mercy was all used up. Grasping her opponent tightly by the front of his jacket, she hauled him into the room's tiny bathroom and shut the door behind her.

"Things are a little different than the last time we met," she said harshly, pulling the man's stun-gun out of his jacket. "This time I can say a few things, too, although you like talking so much that I think I'll let you do most of it."

Taking off her left shoe, she pulled the heel off and took a small hyposprayer from a secret compartment. "I'm going to ask you a few questions now," Yvette continued coldly, "and I'm in no mood for funny answers. I presume you know what I've got in this sprayer?"

The man trembled as he eyed the clear fluid. "N-nitrobarb," he guessed. It had to be. Nitrobarb was the A-number-one most effective truth serum known to man. It was impossible for anyone to lie under its influence. It also had a fifty percent mortality rate, which was why it was on the proscribed list. Mere possession of it was a capital offense.

Yvette gave him a frozen smile. "I'm glad you said that; I dislike admitting to a felony. Now then, I can administer what I have in this hyposprayer to you, or you can talk voluntarily. The choice is entirely up to you. Which will it be?"

"You can put it away. I'll talk," the man said, cradling his right wrist tenderly with his other hand. "I never wanted any trouble, honest. I'm just trying to do a job."

"Is attacking innocent women in their staterooms part of your job?" Yvette sneered. "Let me have the whole story. Who are you and what's your connection with Dak Lehman?"

"My name's Myerson. My partners and I are with Cosmos Investigations."

"A detective?" This unexpected news made Yvette knit her brow in perplexity. "Can you prove that?"

"My ID card's in my jacket pocket." He started to reach for it with his left hand, but Yvette waved his gun at him and he froze in mid-motion.

"I'll get it," she said, and reached into his pocket for

95

his wallet. Sure enough, she found the identification card, together with photo and retinal pattern, stating that Rolf Myerson was a licensed investigative agent under the laws of the planet Largo. This was a development she did not like at all.

"I still don't see where it says you have the right to break and enter."

"Do *you* have that right?" Myerson glared at her.

"I have the gun," Yvette said coolly, "which at the moment gives me the right. I'm not here to argue ethics. I want to know why you were after Dak Lehman."

"His wife hired us to look after him. She . . ."

"Wife? He said nothing to me about any wife."

"Some married men neglect details like that. They were going to be divorced anyway. The two of them own equal shares in the computer firm, though he was the nominal head of the corporation. Gospozha Lehman heard a few rumors that her husband was coming to Vesa to have a secret meeting with someone and sell corporate secrets that would have made her stock in the company worthless. So she hired us to keep an eye on her husband and make sure that no such deals took place."

"But wouldn't he have been cutting his own throat? If the corporate stock became worthless, wouldn't that ruin him as well?"

"He had managed to accumulate, under a variety of other names, a large portfolio of holdings. We thought he felt he could afford to make this spiteful gesture."

"Does he hate his wife that much?"

"In the initial divorce proceedings he's accused her of numerous infidelities. She hasn't denied any of them, so far as I know." Myerson's voice was flat; Gospozha Lehman may have bought his time and services, but not his loyalty.

Yvette considered this latest development. Despite the fact that she'd been unprepared for it, it did seem to make a good deal of sense. Myerson's men had always been primarily concerned with Dak; they had not paid any attention to Yvette until she started seeing the man they were following. Even then, they followed a very cautious approach, trying merely to scare her off when they were afraid she might be getting too close to Dak. She remembered how easily they could have killed her in her suite if they had wanted to do so.

And she remembered all the little discrepancies in Dak's behavior. When she had asked him about other women in his life he had skated neatly around the question—and she had known then he was covering something up. Again, all the little false starts and hesitations in their conversations, as though there were some secret he wanted to tell her but was afraid to reveal. Having a wife—a mean, vindictive, unfaithful woman—back on Largo could very well have been preying on his conscience as he charmed a lovely widow aboard the *Empress Irene*.

The more she thought about it, the more she realized that Myerson's story was probably the truth. *Damn!* she thought. *I was so hoping he'd turn out to be one of the killers. I would have loved to bash his brains out against a wall.*

"What's happened to Gospodin Lehman now?" she asked, trying to keep her voice as even and emotionless as before. "Why did he leave his hotel?"

"You know as much about that as I do. The last we know, Lansky saw him boarding a jit with a friend he met in one of the casinos. Lansky overheard something about a private party, but he didn't know where it was. He tried following, but these damned jits are so elusive that he lost him. Then this morning we find that he vanished last night completely, taking all his worldly possessions with him—which means I'll lose out on my fee for this deal. Gospozha Lehman'll never pay us for losing him."

He looked straight into Yvette's face. "If you ask me, I think we've both been bummed. I think he made his contact and vanished into the night, literally, leaving you and me both holding the bag."

"Yeah," Yvette said cynically. "But I think you and your two friends had better get off Vesa fast, on the next ship to anywhere. I have your stunner, now, and I know how to use it. Next time I see any of your ugly faces, I will. You can take that as a promise." She tucked the hyposprayer back into the heel of her shoe, turned and walked out of the hotel room. Within seconds she was in an elevator tube going down to the seventh level. If Myerson should decide to come looking for her, he would expect her to go up to the lobby.

The hallway on the seventh floor was an exact duplicate of that on the fourth. Tucking the detective's stungun inside her purse, Yvette paced up and down the carpeted hall, much as she'd seen her brother do any number of times in the past. Jules always said he thought better on his feet, but after trying it for a while Yvette came to the conclusion that it only tired out the legs without aiding the brain. Finally she sat crosslegged on the floor and leaned back against the wall.

Myerson's theory would have been a logical one, if that was all there was to the situation. But Yvette knew there was more than that. Dak's disappearance fit too closely into the pattern that had already been established over the past twenty years. A person comes to Vesa, then suddenly vanishes without leaving. All worldly possessions vanish with him. Of course, Dak Lehman could have bought a ticket under an assumed name if he felt that he was being followed . . . but again, this disappearance matched too well with all the others. They couldn't *all* have been selling corporate secrets!

Yvette sighed. She had been hoping so much that Myerson and company had been with the killers; it would have solved a lot of problems and given her new leads. She would tell the Head about Myerson when she got back and his license would be revoked for unethical conduct, but for now she was right back at the start again. Dak was gone, she was untouched, and there was not the faintest clue as to who was responsible for what was happening.

Absolutely nothing!

CHAPTER 9

The Not-So-Great Escape

Jules did not return to his hotel room following his narrow escape from the warehouse. To do so, he knew, would be tantamount to suicide. The Chandakhari he had worked with would have recognized him in the melee, and it would be a simple matter for them to check his work records and discover his address. He mentally wrote off that room as a loss; nothing of any great importance was kept there, and they would find no clues to his real identity if they searched it. All his crucial supplies were kept in a public locker at the spaceport terminal.

He was able to hail a passing jit as he raced out of the warehouse, and vanished into one of the traffic tunnels before any of the people chasing him had even emerged from the building. For the moment he was safe, but he could continue to be so only as long as he kept a couple of jumps ahead of the opposition. Leaning back in his seat, he let the gentle swaying motion of the jit relax his body, which was still tense from the surges of adrenalin. Once he had calmed the physical part of him he turned to the mental.

Georges duChamps would have to disappear, there was no question about it. He hated having to desert Laz Fizcono when the foreman was already shorthanded, but his duty to the Empire came first. Certainly he could not show up for work without inviting the same kind of "accident" that had befallen Rask.

It was equally certain that he would have to leave Vesa. These killers obviously had a widespread conspiracy that enveloped the whole moon, and they would not take kindly to being spied upon. They would turn Vesa upside down in their efforts to find him and, with his distinctive DesPlainian body, he couldn't disguise himself well enough to ensure anonymity.

He toyed with the thought of joining forces with Yvette,

now that his cover in the lower part of Vesa's society was broken. He knew where she was supposed to be staying, and it would be easy enough to get in touch with her. The thought of working together with her was a warming one; they had always been very close, and they worked at their best as a team when they could bounce ideas off one another. And with the killers now looking for him so avidly, the two of them could set a trap and catch some of them. A quick shot of nitrobarb would then help them track down the rest of the mob.

But after some thought he vetoed that idea. Yvette was in the middle of her own investigation; she had her own goals and her own cover identity. It would not be fair of him to interrupt her work just because he'd messed up his own assignment. They had agreed to try a two-pronged attack on the problem in the hopes of solving it that much faster. It still was a sound strategy, if he worked it right.

Besides, he had learned something crucial in the warehouse. Every single one of the murderers assembled there had been a Chandakhar male. Some of them were rather old, and a few, like Radapur, were quite young. Obviously there was some way killers were recruited into this conspiracy, and just as obviously the recruitment was occurring down on the surface of Chandakha. Clearing out all the murders on Vesa would do no good if the factory for producing more of them was left untouched. Chandakha, then, would have to be his next stop. But he would need some help.

He went to the spaceport, got his things from the locker and checked into a nearby hotel. The instant he was alone he activated his room's vidphone and placed an intrasystem call down to a very private number on Chandakha.

After a minute the connection was made, and the screen lit up with the face of a very attractive lady. She also appeared to be a native of Chandakha; she had a dark complexion, brown eyes and long black hair that had just the slightest tipping of gray to it. There were a few lines of responsibility and worry to her face, but they enhanced rather than subtracted from her beauty. Her age could be anywhere from thirty-five to sixty, it was impossible to tell. This would be Marask Kantana, the Service's chief for Chandakha and Vesa.

"Who's there?" she asked peering into her screen, for Jules had kept the video part of his transmission turned off. "What do you want?"

Jules said only one word: "Wombat."

The effect of that word on Kantana was startling. She had been given prior warning that agents Wombat and Periwinkle would be conducting investigations in her area, and that she was to give them all the assistance they required. Even had she not been told in advance, however, the effect would have been the same; those two code names were legendary in the Service, and commanded instant obedience. From a proud woman used to issuing orders, Kantana's visage shifted to one of complete subservience. "What can I do for you?" she asked.

"I'm on Vesa at the moment and I need to get down to Chandakha without being seen. The spaceport will be watched. What do you suggest?"

"There's my private ship," Kantana replied without hesitation. "I could fly up to Vesa for the day, and you could come back packed in my trunk—at least until we got you inside the ship."

"Smooth." Jules decided instantly that he liked this woman. She thought quickly, and had a no-nonsense approach to her job. *No wonder the Head spoke so highly of her,* he thought.

They arranged the details of the pickup in code, though Jules strongly doubted whether the murderers had the capacity to intercept or interpret this call. They had shown no previous inclination to get involved on a political level, preferring to commit their crimes in as quiet and businesslike a manner as possible. Then, when the call was over, Jules leaned back on his bed to rest and think.

Six hours later, Gospozha Kantana's personal spacecraft docked on Vesa. She took her luggage, which consisted of a small briefcase and a large trunk, to a hotel room that was customarily set aside for her periodic trips to the moon. She left her things in the room and went out for a couple of hours' recreation at the casino.

When she returned to her room, Jules was waiting for her. She gave him a polite nod of the head and sat down in a chair in one corner of the room. It would be up to Jules to speak first.

"I've been going over these," he began, holding up a couple of spools of tape. He had requested that she bring up what files the Service had on the seven Chandakhari he had worked with. "I think I've discovered a common pattern to them, and I'd like your advice on the matter."

"My office is at your complete disposal, as you know."

Jules shifted his weight on the bed where he sat. "Each of these men had a criminal record before coming to Vesa. Each came from a large family, of which he was either the sole or principal support—even Radapur, who was only about twenty Earth years old."

"None of those facts is at all unusual on Chandakha," Kantana said matter-of-factly. "It is not a pleasant place to live. It's a tropical world, and only one of its five continents is habitable by humans; the rest are hellholes and breeding grounds for insects and plagues. Even the one continent where we can live is ravaged periodically by rainstorms, droughts, floods and insect swarms.

"Whichever bureaucrat came up with the idea of colonizing Chandakha decided that it could best be done by using people who were already accustomed to these problems. As a result, most of the colonists—my ancestors included—were recruited from the Indian subcontinent of Earth and transplanted here. Some of our customs were brought over, some were dropped and new ones were created. The caste system, which lingered on in India even after it was officially abolished, is almost nonexistent here, though you still find traces every so often. But one problem that took root here was overpopulation, which we nearly had licked by the twenty-second century. We have it worse now than it's ever been.

"It's not uncommon for a married couple here to have twenty or twenty-five children during their lifetime. With modern medicine, most of those survive. At first, there was plenty of land to go around, but we've been here three centuries now. Family parcels are being whittled down, until now the average family is hard-pressed to support itself.

"Many people, fed up with farm life, move into the cities. But it's even worse there. We have little heavy industry, since all the resorces of this continent are used to feed ourselves, and the other continents can't be mined. Jobs are scarce, but people have to live. Crime is the one profession they can turn to. It's been estimated that at least one person in ten on Chandakha makes most of his living by illegal means. In the cities, that ratio can be as high as four in ten."

Jules was flabbergasted by this revelation. "But who do they steal from?"

"The honest people. Each other. Anyone and everyone." Though Kantana's voice was even, the look behind her eyes showed her true feelings. This was a sympathetic woman who had long borne the burden of these people's problems even though, in her exalted position as chief of the local SOTE office, she could have ignored them.

Jules was shaking his head. "I find it hard to believe that conditions like these could exist in the Empire today. The Emperor can't condone these things." He remembered his one meeting with His Imperial Majesty Stanley Ten—an old man, yes, but sharp-witted and deeply caring for the people he ruled.

Kantana's voice was without bitterness. "The Emperor is very busy and very far away. Chandakha is very peaceful, no threat to him or the Empire. When a man rules over thirteen hundred planets he has to govern by crisis; the quiet problems get overlooked. Besides, the problem has only really begun to emerge in the last fifty years; we've had a string of undistinguished dukes who've fumbled around without accomplishing anything. The present duke is only thirteen, and. . . ." She stopped abruptly. "I'm terribly sorry. You didn't come here to listen to my problems or Chandakha's. You've . . . we've got a case to solve, and the sooner we get onto that, the better."

Jules put his shock at the conditions on Chandakha to the back of his mind. Kantana was right; they had work to do. "What I'm thinking," he said, "is that there is a regular program of recruitment going on. This conspiracy picks out people who already have criminal tendencies and who have large families to support—men who are desperate enough to do anything for money. They can be trained to be callous about anything, even wholesale murder, if the incentive's right."

"If ever there was a recruiter's paradise for that sort of thing," Kantana agreed, "Chandakha is it. In fact, as far as I can see, the hardest part of a recruiter's job would be choosing from an almost limitless number of candidates."

Jules brooded on that for a bit. "Then what we have to do," he said at last, "is to make sure I'm an irresistible candidate for them."

Before leaving Vesa, Jules phoned and had an ad placed in the personal column of the major newsroll:

> Chandakha sings a siren song.
> The natives are restless.
> Frenchie

Yvette would know from that that her brother had gone down to the planet's surface, and that Chandakhari were somehow involved. He hated being so mysterious, but she had her own independent investigation to perform, and he didn't want to prejudice her findings. At least she would know he was all right; if she had any further questions she could contact Kantana, just as he did.

The transfer to Kantana's ship was accomplished smoothly, with Jules riding inside her capacious trunk. The trunk was carried aboard ship through the passenger ramp; Jules was jarred a bit, but he got past any possible spies at the spaceport without detection. As Kantana piloted them down on the short flight to Chandakha, she and Jules discussed his upcoming transformation into a leading criminal of the planet.

The physical part would be the hardest. Jules' light brown hair, fair skin and gray eyes would never pass muster but Kantana assured him she had makeup experts at her disposal who could administer skin and hair dyes that would last for several weeks. Service opthalmologists could also dye his eyes temporarily to a more passable brown. As for his distinctively DesPlainian physique, Kantana assured him that the standard garb on Chandakha was a loosefitting garment cut like a caftan. By taking certain pills to promote water retention, Jules could make most of his musculature look like just plain flab. Sleep tapes helped him learn the local dialect in six nights.

Being more familiar with the culture of the planet, Kantana invented Jules' background. He would be Har Koosman, twenty-eight, a family man with a wife and nine children to support. He had lived all his life in Calpuna, the second largest city on the planet, and had been in and out of jails since he was sixteen—she could fake the records for that easily enough, and the local police would cooperate with her fully. Two months ago, he had gotten into his most serious trouble by trying to break into the estate of the Baron of Calpuna and steal his jewels. He was discovered and captured—but not before he had killed two of the Baron's guards attempting to escape. He was imprisoned in solitary confinement in Calpuna for a while, but managed to escape. He had just been recaptured and the Service, acting at the request of the Baron, had stepped in to assist the local police. Koosman was now being transferred to the Imperial prison at Bhangora, Chandakha's largest city, where security would be a lot stricter. "And," as Kantana pointed out, "where no one would be expected to know a criminal from Calpuna."

Har Koosman paced his small cell impatiently. He had been locked in with a man named Passar, a tiny man about forty years old with the face of a weasel and eyes permanently hardened to criminal activities. "Passar has connections all through the underworld," Kantana had told Jules. "If he doesn't know how to get you through to the recruiters, no one will."

"I've got to get out of here," Jules muttered as he paced. He turned to look at Passar. "You know this area better than I do, you must know a way out."

The older man chuckled grimly. "If I knew, would I still be here?"

"There must be a way out. No prison is escape proof."

"True enough, *tovarishch*. Men have escaped from here

before. But they thought up their plans over the course of months. You just got here this morning, what can you expect?"

Jules shook his head. "I've got a wife and nine kids, two aged parents and a brother-in-law, none of whom can support themselves. I'm alone in a strange city, without a friend to my name, being held on a charge of murder. What am I going to do?" Jules sat down on the edge of the crude bunk he'd been provided and buried his face in his hands.

"I'll tell you what you won't do," said Passar, becoming annoyed. "You won't bore me any more with the tearful story of your problems. I've been in and out of jails for thirty years, and I've had so many people sob on my shoulder that it's permanently soggy. Every cell in this building has men who, by their own admission, shouldn't be there, and each has a tale as pitiful as yours. This cell is three meters wide and four long; if you intend to share it peacefully with me, you will keep your damned mouth shut and stop your wail of self-pity."

"Why you miserable little bastard," Jules let his anger flare. "How dare you talk to me like that? I'll kill you!" And with that, he surged off his cot and over to where his cellmate was seated.

His large powerful hands closed over the smaller man's throat. To Passar it felt as though the newcomer was using all his strength in a murderous rage, though in truth Jules was using but a tenth of what he could have. He certainly didn't want to kill Passar, though the other had to think he would.

Passar had just enough warning and enough air left in his lungs to yell for the guard. He tried beating Jules off, but his blows were very light and struck uselessly on the attacker's toughened hide. Jules shifted position slightly, in what looked like an attempt to gain a better grip but what was actually a chance to let Passar get more air in his lungs to scream. The weaselly little criminal did so with gratifying volume.

"What's going on here?" came a voice from outside the cell. A large, burly guard stood there, his stun-gun drawn and aimed at the participants in the struggle. He was trying to get a clear shot at Jules, but in another second he would fire at both men, on the theory that stunning both of them would ease the problem and allow him time to sort out the bodies in peace afterwards.

Before he could fire, though, Jules suddenly dropped Passar and lunged with his arm through the bars at the guard. He caught the man's gunhand and, with a vicious yank, pulled the guard towards him. The man hit his head hard against the metal bars and was knocked unconscious. He would have slumped to the floor had not Jules held his body upright. The stun-gun dropped from the guard's limp hand onto the floor of the cell, but Jules was much more interested in the other gun the guard had carried—a Mark Twenty blaster. Stretching his other hand between the bars, he pulled the heavy weapon out of the guard's holster. Then he let the man's body fall to the ground.

Wasting no time, Jules turned the blaster's sizzling beam on the lock mechanism of the cell. Within three seconds the lock had been burned away. The DesPlainian kicked open the door, picked up the stun-gun as well and turned back to the startled Passar, who had watched the action while cowering in his bunk. "Thanks," Jules told him. "I needed a commotion to draw the guard's attention, and it had to seem realistic." He stepped out of the cell. "Be seeing you."

"What about me?" Passar called after him.

Jules shrugged. "Door's open. You're free to try a break, too, if you want."

Passar's weasel brain was working overtime. "You'll never be able to get out of here alone, and neither will I. You don't know the layout and I don't have a gun. Together, though, we stand a chance."

Though Jules pretended to consider that, it was actually exactly what he'd hoped for. The entire escape scene had been choreographed for Passar's benefit, with the guard being part of the drama. Ordinarily the man would never have stood within arm's length of the prisoners like that, and he would have stunned first and asked questions later. But the breakout had to look realistic enough so that Passar wouldn't smell a trap. Jules needed Passar, all

107

right. Not to help him escape, as the old man thought—Jules could have walked unmolested out of the prison, and he'd memorized its floor plan; instead, he needed Passar as a passport to whoever was recruiting the murderers.

"*Khorosho,* but hurry it up," he snarled. "The alarms must have gone off in the front office by now."

"Of course they have, the instant that door was opened," Passar said, racing out of the cell. "Let's go this way."

"But the front entrance is that way," Jules protested, pointing in the opposite direction. "I remember that much from when they brought me in."

"Sure—and that's exactly the direction they'll expect us to go. This way's the laundry chute; they won't look for us in there right away." He pulled at Jules' sleeve. "Come on."

Jules followed the older man down the narrow corridors of cells. They passed plenty of other prisoners who watched them go by silently. Some of the men gave Jules the high sign as he went by, wishing him luck and wishing they could be along. None of them would utter a sound or do anything to ruin his chances of escape. Such was the camaraderie of prison life.

The sound of running footsteps came from the hall ahead of them. Passar found them a small side door and they turned into it just as a group of guards appeared at the far end of the hallway. While Jules and his partner scarcely dared breathe, the squad ran past their hiding place and back down the corridor the pair had just come from. Passar waited several seconds to make sure they'd all be gone, then burst out of the room and continued on his way. Jules was right behind him, brandishing his weapons menacingly.

They came to the laundry chute. Passar opened it up and slid down it without hesitation; again, Jules was right on his tail. Together the two men tumbled down the metal slide and landed with a soft *whoosh* amid a pile of smelly old prison uniforms. Climbing quickly out of the bin, they looked around.

It was Passar who found what they needed—some guard's uniforms that had been stained and were sent here for quick cleaning. Jules found one his size and was starting to get into it when an inmate—a trusty, no doubt—came around the corner. Before he could do much more than register his surprise, Jules had given him a light stun. As he fell to the floor, Jules continued dressing.

There were no uniforms in Passar's size, so they hastily devised a plan. "I'll be a guard transporting you to another cell block," Jules said. "If we play it right, no one'll give us a second glance. Which way do we go?"

"That way's out." Passar pointed to a small locked door that led out the side of the laundry area. A short blast from Jules' gun and the door was no longer a barrier. The two men walked out into the yard, Passar a little ahead with Jules holding the stun-gun on him.

There was great confusion in the yard as guards ran around everywhere, trying to look as though they did not know exactly what was going on. Actually, Jules' and Passar's actions had been monitored each step of the way, and all the guards had been told that the breakout was scheduled. Their major concern was to see that none of the other prisoners took advantage of the situation and tried any breaks on their own.

A number of guard cars had been scattered about the yard. Jules and Passar took the one that looked the fastest and got in. "We'll never get out the gates, though," Passar was muttering. "They close automatically at an escape attempt, and can only be opened from a guard station."

"Stop sniveling," Jules snapped at him. "I'm a guard now myself, remember? And I've got a couple of guns."

As he drove up to the gate, he said, "Get down on the floor where they can't see you. I've got an idea." Passar did as he was told, and Jules stopped in front of the closed steel gate. A guard came over to him and recognized him instantly as the man he was supposed to let escape. Nevertheless, he had to make it look good.

"Where are you going?" he asked.

"The warden wants me to patrol the perimeter," Jules said. "He thinks they may have found a way to get outside the walls, and he wants me driving around to see if I can spot anything." He also winked at the guard, a gesture Passar could not see from his position on the floor.

The guard gave an imperceptible nod and said, "Khorosho, pass through." With a wave of his hand he signaled his companion in the booth to open the gate. As the monstrous steel doors swung wide, Jules gave him a wave of his hand and drove quickly outside. He started around the wall until he was out of sight of the sentry, then tore off across the open countryside in the direction of Bhangora.

Passar climbed up off the floor to sit beside Jules again. "I didn't think it'd work," he said. "I thought you had to have special papers or something to get out."

"Aah, we got them so confused right now they don't know what they're doing," Jules excused.

"In any event, we won't have more than a couple of minutes before they realize we're gone," Passar said. "Better gun it to Bhangora. That way." He pointed, and Jules drove obediently in the indicated direction. From here on, he'd have to let Passar lead him if he intended to get where he wanted to go.

Three minutes later, Passar, who'd been checking out the window behind them, said, "They're on our tail."

Indeed they were. At least a dozen police cruisers were chasing them, making a pretense at trying to recapture them. Jules hit the accelerator as hard as he could and the escapees' car zoomed ahead at maximum speed. Jules' reflexes were superb, and he drove the car like an extension of himself. On the seat beside him, he knew that Passar was sitting white-knuckled at the recklessness of his driving. *All part of the atmosphere,* Jules thought, smiling inwardly.

If this were a real jailbreak, of course, there would be roadblocks ahead of them as well as pursuit from behind. There would be copters and personal flyers spotting them from the air, possibly even dropping small gas bombs. But this break was programmed to succeed, and it couldn't be made too difficult. At the same time, those cars to their rear had to be used so that it wouldn't look too easy to the suspicious Passar. The main point was that events had to move so fast that he wouldn't have time to think; he would have to accept events at their face value.

For five minutes they zipped along country roads and through open fields where families of peasants were tending their crops. After that, though, they reached the edges of the city. Houses became bigger and more closely spaced; other types of buildings—factories, shops, grocery stores—began to make their appearance. People were more prevalent, too, walking along the sides of the road, carrying bundles, engaging in commerce. Despite his desire to hurry, Jules had to slow down to avoid hitting any of the pedestrians.

"We'll have to ditch the car soon," Passar said. "They'll have tracers on us in a little while. We're getting into a neighborhood I know, though, so we'll be able to find hiding spots until some of the heat's off." He began directing Jules along the proper course.

They were definitely within the city now, and Jules' speed had been reduced practically to a crawl. The houses to either side were dirty and ill-kept. Windows were shattered more often than not. Children played naked in the streets, their shouts and squeals echoing down the canyons of buildings. Wash hung from lines that were strung across the streets themselves, sometimes only a meter or two above the tops of passing vehicles. The clothes could not get completely clean that way, but no one seemed to care very much.

The people living in the houses, though, were the lucky ones. The sidewalks were jammed sometimes two or three deep with people and their belongings. Tattered old blankets stretched out on the ground served some people as mattresses. Others lay down just in the hard-packed dirt or mud. Small fires were set right out at the edge of the street, where soup kettles seemed to be constantly boiling. Everywhere was the look of starvation and apathy. Jules shuddered to think of it, but kept his disgust hidden; as Har Koosman, such sights should be as familiar to him as his own face in the mirror.

At length they came to a spot where the street was frankly impassable. The press of people had become so great that they simply overflowed the sidewalks into the thoroughfare, and no vehicle could hope to get through. Jules looked at Passar for advice, but the latter only shrugged. "We'd've had to go on foot from here, anyhow," the older man said.

Jules stripped off his guard uniform to the caftan beneath it and the two escapees jumped from their car, leaving it stopped in the middle of the street to be stolen by anyone passing by. Passar started running through the crowd, slipping between the people who jammed the path as though he were a boneless figure. There obviously was an art to dodging through crowds like this, but it was one that Jules had not mastered. Try though he did to follow Passar's motions exactly, he found himself knocking people over or stepping on their feet as he raced along after his companion. Every few meters he would have to leap over the body of someone sleeping or, possibly, dead on the sidewalk. How he managed to keep Passar in sight while maneuvering through the throng he was never sure afterwards; somehow, though, desperation gave him the extra edge he needed.

Passar never looked back to see whether Jules was following him or not. He assumed, probably, that Jules was as adept at street running as he was, and consequently didn't see how clumsy his partner really was. That might have broken Jules' cover right there. But Passar's attention was focused on two things—first, to get them lost in the crowd as thoroughly as possible so that the police following them would not be able to find them; and second, to take them to a place of refuge.

At last, Passar turned off the main streets and into a back alley that ran between two rows of buildings. He raced about a third of the way down the row, then descended a short flight of stairs to a basement door. Jules broke free of the crowd in the streets and, with an extra burst of speed, managed to catch up with the older man enough to make him think he'd been right behind all the time.

Passar gave two quick raps on the door, paused, gave another rap, paused again, then gave one more rap. The door swung inward, and Passar and Jules slid inside into a darkened room. At first, Jules could not see a thing, his

112

eyes being accustomed to the glare of the light outside; but as his eyes became adjusted to the gloom he could see that they were in a storage cellar. Racks of bottles ran the length of the room, with large stacks of boxes scattered in the aisles between the racks.

"Where are we?" Jules asked.

"Safe," Passar said ambiguously. "It don't pay you to know more than that."

Jules took the hint and shut up. The place must be a bar or cocktail lounge, judging from all the bottles piled around. It was also a hiding place of some repute, because the door had opened immediately at Passar's knocks, indicating it was constantly manned. On a planet where crime was as rife as on Chandakha, criminals would have systems of hideouts. It was also likely, Jules thought, that they would have to pay a price for their sanctuary.

"Oh, it's you, Passar," said the man who'd opened the door—a large, burly fellow with a face that had suffered through a thousand barroom brawls. "Funny; I didn't think we'd be seeing you for quite some time. We'd heard you'd found another hangout, eh?" He laughed at his own small joke.

Passar joined him in the laughter. "Well, it seems they didn't like my company, so they let me out a little early— me and my friend here." He hesitated a moment, then added, "Ah, the only trouble is that we packed in such a hurry that we neglected to bring our wallets."

"That is a shame," the doorman agreed solemnly. "Gospodin Tuhlman will have to be apprised of this."

"Of course," Passar said as the other man pressed an intercom button. Turning to Jules, Passar said, "Don't worry, I know Tuhlman pretty well. He won't turn us out. There's always little odd jobs that need doing. We can trade services for our keep. Everything'll be all right." And he winked at Jules.

CHAPTER 10

Games

Yvette spent most of the day after her talk with Myerson wandering aimlessly around Vesa, trying to get her thoughts in order. *Think, girl,* she commanded herself. *You're behaving like a schoolchild. Don't let your brain turn to jelly. Think!*

There was one weak link in the chain of killings, one spot where the killers would have to surface—the victim's hotel. Spaceship tickets could be cashed in over the phone and the money deposited to a blind bank account, but somebody would have to go to the hotel and remove the victim's belongings personally. The killers would have to have the compliance of some person or persons on the hotel staff to be able to clean out a room so thoroughly and so quickly. And they would need the assistance of someone to arrange all the checkouts. Which meant widespread corruption throughout the staffs of each tourist hotel on the moon.

At 0130 hours that night she walked calmly into the lobby of the Soyuz Hotel, where Dak had been staying. Even at this hour there were large numbers of people crossing the lobby or sitting around in chairs reading the local newsrolls. The nightclerk was on duty behind the desk, sorting some incoming mail.

Yvette strode confidently up to the desk, her houppelande swirling as she moved. "Were you on duty here last night?" she asked.

"Yes, I was," the man replied without looking up from his task.

"I'm told that a man named Dak Lehman checked out exactly twenty-four hours ago."

"It's possible."

"I'd like to know some more of the details about his departure."

"Gospozha, so many people check in and out that

114

I. . . ." He stopped suddenly as he looked up from his work. Yvette was holding the stun-gun she had taken from Myerson, and the muzzle was only ten centimeters from the clerk's face. The bulk of her body hid the gun from the view of the rest of the people in the lobby.

"What is this, a robbery?"

"No, as I said, I only want some information, and I think you can give it to me. Is there somewhere private we can go?"

"Th-there's the office back here," the clerk said, never taking his eyes off the barrel of the gun.

"Good; I suggest we go there at once. I also suggest you make no sudden movements. I am, by nature, a very nervous person, and this stun-gun is set on eight. It would paralyze you for days at least, with the possibility of permanent crippling. I'm sure you wouldn't like that, would you?"

"No, gospozha, not at all," the man assured her. "Follow me, please."

He led her into a small, well-appointed office behind the front desk. She closed the door behind them and motioned for him to sit down in the easy chair. When he'd done so, she took a length of rope out of her purse and proceeded to tie him up quite securely.

"Now that we've got the preliminaries out of the way I can explain the rules of the game," Yvette said coolly. "I'll ask you questions and you'll provide me with answers. You have three alternatives—you can either lie, remain silent or tell the truth. I also have three alternatives—I can either accept what you've said, kick you where it hurts most or use my gun. *Very* simple rules, don't you agree?"

The clerk was sweating profusely, and could only nod his head in reply.

Yvette had a fourth alternative, namely the nitrobarb that was still concealed in her shoe; but using it on so insignificant a cog in the killers' machine would be pointless. One doesn't use a blaster to kill gnats.

"All right, then, we'll begin. Did Dak Lehman actually check out last night?"

The man wet his lips with his tongue. "I can show you on the records that. . . ."

"I saw the records yesterday afternoon. They don't prove a damn thing. You were *there*, gospodin. Did Dak Lehman personally check out of this hotel?"

The clerk was on a spot and he knew it. This ferocious young lady meant business. "Not personally, no. A friend of his checked out for him."

"A friend, eh? Did this *friend* also go up to the room and clear out all of Gospodin Lehman's belongings?"

"Yes, and he also paid the bill. Look, he had a key so I thought it would be all right."

"Yes, I'm sure you did. This *friend*—had you ever seen him before?"

"What do you mean?"

"I'm asking the questions here. I would think my meaning was perfectly clear; I used only two words with more than one syllable." She began limbering up her foot as though preparing to kick him in a very sensitive area. The man watched her nervously.

"Uh, yes, I had seen him before."

Yvette cocked her head. "Talking to you, *tovarishch*, is like pulling teeth. I think we'll add a new rule to the game. It's called completeness of answer, and the way it works is that you try to answer each question as fully as you can, without making me ask a dozen to get the whole story. Each time your answer is not as full as I'd like it, I break one of your fingers. That's known as incentive. Now, would you like to try that last answer one more time?"

The poor clerk was sweating blood now. "Yes, I'd seen him before. He comes in here fairly regularly—two, three, sometimes four times a week. I don't know his name, though, honest."

"And does he always check other people out of their rooms?"

"Always," the man nodded. "The first thing I know about it is when he comes down to the desk with all their luggage packed. He hands in the key and pays the bill in cash. The hotel doesn't care who checks out as long as the bill's paid."

"No, I don't suppose it does. He must be a remarkably friendly fellow to have so many people trusting him with their belongings, don't you think? No need to answer that, it was just rhetorical. Tell me, though, don't you think it's strange that he does this so often?"

"Yes, I do. But I don't think it's any of my business."

"How much is this *friend* paying you to think it's none of your business?"

"Fifty rubles each time. But listen, I've got a wife and kids to support, I need. . . ."

"That answer is getting a little *too* full thank you. I'm not interested in your personal problems, although I am interested in your morality." She stared straight into the man's eyes. "You know what's happening to all these guests of yours, don't you? The ones who never check out for themselves?"

The clerk took a long, deep breath. There was no point holding any more back—this woman obviously knew most of the story anyway. She was toying with him, seeming to enjoy every little twist of the psychological knife she had stuck in him. "Yes," he sighed. "They're being murdered. It's a fact of life here on Vesa, and most people accept it. It's only tourists who are killed, never us natives. We accept it."

"Accepting it is one thing, but you're actually *helping* it. How does that make you feel? How can you go home to a wife and kids you supposedly love and yet know that you have a hand in killing innocent people? How can you face them?"

The man shrugged as best he could while tied up. "If I didn't do it, somebody else would. Why shouldn't I get the money out of it?"

Yvette sighed with exasperation. That rationalization had been in existence as long as moral cowardice itself. There was probably at least one corrupt desk clerk in every hotel on Vesa. There was no point arguing this matter further; to the best of this man's limited moral vision he had done no wrong. She decided to change her tack. "Don't the police ever bother you about these disappearances?"

"No, why should they? They're under orders not to interfere."

Under orders? That brought Yvette right back to the

point that had initially been brought up in the Head's office. "There's only one person who can give the police an order like that, isn't there? The Marchioness."

"That's what I understand. Look, I'm not really a part of this whole thing, I'm only paid to look the other way. I'm no murderer, I don't know anything about them. All I do know is what I hear gossiped around, and people say that the Marchioness has given 'hands off' orders. That's all I can tell you, honest. I don't know anything else."

Yvette was inclined to believe him. This clerk was just a minor part of the operation; he wouldn't be privy to the conspiracy's inner secrets. He had given her several leads and confirmed a lot of what she'd already suspected. She shouldn't press him for more.

"All right," she said aloud. "I'll tell you what I'm going to do. Because you've been so good at playing this game, I won't hurt you." The man's body visibly sagged with relief. "I will, however, have to keep you out of the way for a while, so that you don't tell anyone about my visit here. I'm turning the setting on this stunner down to seven; you'll be out for approximately thirty-six hours and groggy for a little bit after that, but there'll be no permanent effects. I'd suggest, though, that you move to some other planet and find a new job at once, if you know what's good for you—preferably an honest job."

The man started to protest, but to no avail. Yvette was already squeezing the trigger. The clerk slumped bonelessly in his chair and Yvette stood up, put the gun back into her purse and walked casually out of the office.

Looks like I'll have to go right to the top, she thought. Flagging down a jit, she headed back for her hotel so that she could get some sleep before paying a call tomorrow on Marchioness Gindri.

In most places, the social calendar of someone as high ranking as a marchioness would have made it impossible for Yvette to get an appointment sooner than two or three days away. In the hierarchy of nobility, marquises ranked just below dukes, who ruled individual planets. A marquis

118

was the lord of a continent—or, in the case of Vesa, a moon—and had a vast territory to oversee. The responsibility was enormous, and the amount of time available for private audiences was therefore limited.

Yvette knew well enough the weight of such nobility. Her father, Etienne d'Alembert, was the Duke of DesPlaines; because he was usually busy managing the Circus—and its clandestine activities for the Emperor—the planet was usually run by Yvette's older brother Robert who, as heir to the title of DesPlaines, went by the honorific of the next lower rank, marquis. Robert was an anomaly among d'Alemberts—a man who preferred the quiet harassment of running a world to the excitement of traveling with the Circus—and the Duke was glad of the opportunity to dump the responsibility on the shoulders of his heir. Yvette knew how strenuous the governing of a planet could be from having seen her brother in action, and she fully expected Marchioness Gindri to be as busy.

Instead, she found that—with the offer of a small bribe —she could convince the Marchioness's appointments secretary to schedule her for that very afternoon. She was a little surprised, but pleased with the fast action. She told the secretary that she was interested in investing some of her considerable fortune on Vesa, and was informed that the Marchioness would be eager to hear her plans.

When she arrived, Yvette found the palace gaudy and pretentious—but she had expected as much. Vesa itself was like that, so why should its ruler be any different? Precious metals, expensive woods and exquisite marbles comprised the setting, with gems inlaid into even the most trivial of objects. The display of opulence and bad taste offended the SOTE agent, but she kept her feelings strictly in line. *Not everyone was raised in a tent,* she reflected. *Tastes differ.*

She found it harder to keep her emotions in check when she was finally ushered into the Marchioness's presence. The meeting took place in the salon, a room as ostentatious as any Yvette had seen. The floor was an abstract pattern of inlaid tiles, the walls were of brown marble and the high-vaulted ceiling was painted in an almost surrealistic design of a spaceship battle that had never taken place. The arched entranceways were supported by pillars a full four meters tall. The room was cluttered with furniture, all of it upholstered in silver-embroidered rose satin and wildly overstuffed.

In the center of the room, draped in pearls, sat the Marchioness Gindri, all one hundred and fifty kilograms of her. Her pasty skin shook whenever she made the slightest movement, like a tubful of jelly. Her eyes were deepset and piggy, her nose large and set flatly against her face. Her mouth seemed intrinsically incapable of closing completely.

Beside and slightly behind the Marchioness's chair stood a man whose face impressed Yvette immediately. His mouth was ringed by a full brown beard and mustache, his eyes were sharp and missed no details as their gaze continually darted about the room. There was a feral intelligence lurking behind those eyes, Yvette decided. The man was dressed in a white tunic-jacket and slacks, with a fist-sized emerald hanging from a gold chain about his neck. In other contexts Yvette would have thought him overweight, but standing beside the Marchioness he looked positively emaciated.

No wonder she's got an empty calendar, Yvette thought. *No one wants anything to do with her.*

Keeping a firm mask over her true feelings, Yvette curtsied and approached to within two meters. As the daughter of a duke and sister of a marquis, she had been schooled in all the courtly graces and could outpoint anyone on etiquette. But Carmen Velasquez was supposed to be a commoner and, despite having a lot of money, was inexperienced at dealing with nobility. Deliberately she made her curtsy awkward and projected a nervousness at being in the Marchioness's presence that she certainly did not feel. "Your Highness . . ." she began fumblingly.

The man standing beside the Marchioness corrected her. "Your Excellency," he prompted.

"Yes, oh, sorry, Your Excellency. I'm sorry, I've never met anyone of your exalted rank before. My name is

120

Carmen Velasquez and I asked to see you because I was wanting to invest a great deal of my money on Vesa and I wanted to discuss various plans."

"Do you like Vesa?" the Marchioness asked. Her voice was quite raspy and seemed to escape from rather than be uttered by, that large mouth and multiple chins.

"Oh, very much, Your Excellency. I've been here a couple of weeks now and I find it fascinating. My husband died recently, leaving me with a considerable fortune, and your moon looks like a good breeding ground for cash. A smart person could make a killing here."

She scrutinized the faces of both people opposite her, but neither reacted to the word "killing." She hadn't expected them to, but anything was worth a try.

"Many fortunes have indeed been made here, gospozha," said the man, "and small ones have been enlarged. There is always room for capital investment. How much were you thinking of investing?"

"Please pardon me, gospodin, but I don't recall having been told your name," Yvette excused. "I don't mean to be rude, but my husband always told me to find out beforehand who you're dealing with."

"Of course, dear lady; the apologies are all mine for not having spoken up sooner. My name is Garst, and I am Her Excellency's First Advisor."

Though her face remained placid, her mind was spinning as she tried to place that name. *Garst. I know I've heard it somewhere before. But where?* "Thank you, Gospodin Garst. I was considering a modest sum to start out with—say, seven or eight million rubles?"

The way Garst's eyes lit up, she could tell he considered that sum to be slightly better than modest. He began eyeing her in much greater detail now, trying to peek behind the figurative mask she was wearing to discover more about this mysterious rich widow. She could almost hear the gears clicking in his brain. Then suddenly, as his eyes were traveling over her body, he froze for the slightest of instants. A scowl flew quickly across his face and disappeared. "That's a very attractive offer from a very attractive DesPlainian," he said. Did she detect an ever-so-slight emphasis on that last word?

"I'm not a DesPlainian, though you're close," she hastened to point out. "I'm originally from Purity, though I saw the error of those ways early enough to leave before becoming thoroughly conditioned. The gravities of the two planets are remarkably similar, though, and lead to similar body structures, so I can understand the confusion."

"My mistake, gospozha. Please forgive the error." His voice was now carefully neutral, giving not the slightest clue to his feelings.

Suddenly Yvette remembered where she'd heard Garst's name before. Dak had mentioned it. He'd said he was going to a private party at the home of someone named Garst, a local VIP. It was the last thing on his agenda the day he . . . disappeared. Myerson had confirmed that Dak had set out to Garst's party, and that was the last anyone had ever seen of him. Suddenly this fellow Garst took on a strange new fascination for Yvette.

He doesn't leave the Marchioness's side, she noticed. It was as though Vesa's ruler depended on him for more than just advice. "I'm glad you find my offer attractive," she said casually. "I know you have plenty of hotels and casinos here already, but you also have so many tourists that I thought one more could always help. To be a little different, I was thinking of subsidizing the construction of a transparent dome up on the actual surface of the moon—with, naturally, transportation tunnels linking it to the rest of Vesa underground. It would be something unique here, and I think the tourists would go for it in a big way."

"The thought of a surface dome has been brought up before," Garst said. "There are, of course, numerous problems to overcome, such as the threat of meteor damage. So far there hasn't been anyone with sufficient capital and incentive to follow through on the idea. Perhaps you will be the first."

They continued to talk for another fifteen minutes, but the conversation quickly became a verbal sparring match between Yvette and the First Advisor. While the Marchioness sat idly by and listened only to what was said, the other two antagonists were carefully measuring each other's words, tones and inflections for hidden meanings and possible weaknesses. It was a serious verbal game of cat-and-mouse, with neither side willing to concede a point to the other. Yvette detailed her "plans" for the dome and Garst promised the Marchioness's support of the project; but below that level, nothing was accomplished other than a suspicious circling.

By the time she had to leave, Yvette had firmed up several of her suspicions. Marchioness Gindri was not the brains behind this conspiracy of murder, that much was certain; Yvette saw her as a silly—and very sad—woman. She might well know what was going on, would almost have to, in fact, to give the police their "hands off" orders; they wouldn't take such orders from anyone less, even the First Advisor, lest they be discovered. But Gindri had neither the cunning to set up such an organization nor the drive to keep it going. That would take someone with a lot more guile and a lot fewer weaknesses.

Garst fit that description perfectly. There was an innate craftiness about him that would allow him to conceive of such a scheme; a coldness that would brush aside all moral inhibitions; and a high position that would allow him to act virtually unchecked.

She was definitely going to have to learn more about this Gospodin Garst—and as quickly as possible!

As soon as the Velasquez woman had left the palace, Garst excused himself from the Marchioness's presence and went to call his lieutenant, Lessin. "Is there any word yet on duChamps?" he asked.

"None," Lessin reported, "but it shouldn't be much longer. I've had an artist do up a composite sketch on his face, and every man we've got here has seen it. I've even sent a copy down to the school, on the off chance he'll show up there."

"Good. There's someone else we may have to check out, a woman named Carmen Velasquez. She also looks to be a DesPlainian, which is what made me suspicious. She came in here with too good an offer, and I think she's fishing for something. She claims to be an ex-Puritan, but I've known a few of them and they're not at all like

123

her. Whoever she is, she's awfully shrewd—too shrewd to be just what she appears."

"Do you want her eliminated?"

Garst shook his head. "No, not yet. There's still the chance that she might be legitimate, and her business deal would be a very good one if we could swing it. But I do want to keep a check on her. She said she's staying at the Hotel Regulus. I want her watched all the time. I want to know where she goes, what she does and who she talks to." *And particularly*, he thought, *whether she contacts a DesPlainian calling himself Georges duChamps. She could be the key to cracking that mystery.*

CHAPTER 11

School for Stranglers

As Passar had told him, everything turned out all right—better than all right, in fact. Jules had not dared hope to be so successful so quickly.

Passar took Jules upstairs and introduced him to Tuhlman, a short, oily man built like a barrel and smelling like a locker room. Tuhlman was full of pointed questions about their escape, which he viewed as nothing short of miraculous. Jules let Passar do most of the talking. Tuhlman would believe the story more if it came from someone he knew—and besides, Passar did such a good job of embellishing it that Jules could hardly recognize their escapades himself. Any slipups he might have made were covered nicely by Passar's exaggerations.

Then came the matter of paying for their sanctuary. Passar was no problem—he had plenty of contacts and could line himself up with a lot of work in no time. But Jules was another matter. Tuhlman questioned him in depth about his past, and Jules answered carefully from the background Chief Kantana had prepared for him. The picture that resulted was that of a man who would be hunted down like an animal if he stayed on Chandakha, who had a large family that he wanted desperately to support, and who would do anything—including killing—to get money. The portrait, Jules hoped, of an ideal recruit for the Vesan conspiracy.

Tuhlman took the bait. He asked Passar to leave the room for a few minutes, and talked to Jules privately about an organization that might help him get offworld and at the same time look after his family. The work they would require of him would be both easy and safe, though Tuhlman was careful not to go too deeply into specifics. He spoke in such glowing terms that Jules was convinced the man got a commission for each recruit he gathered. It was a hard sales pitch to resist, and Jules did not want to. He told Tuhlman he'd be delighted to sign up, and the two men shook hands on the deal. Tuhlman then had Passar and Jules shown to a small room where they had a good hot meal and spent the night.

Bright and early the next morning, two men came and awakened Jules brusquely, rousting him out of bed and telling him to dress quickly. He got only a fast cup of tepid tea as he was rushed out to a waiting copter that took off as soon as he and the men were aboard. The men put a blindfold on him and circled around the city for a while until they were sure his sense of direction had been scrambled, then set off for their destination. Jules asked where they were going and was told bluntly to shut up and mind his own business. The rest of the trip was conducted in silence.

The quiet was just as well. Jules, not having a watch or any artificial method of gauging the time, took advantage of the lack of conversation to count his own heartbeats. He had to find out how far away from Bhangora the training center was, and that biological rhythm would be his only clue.

About an hour and a half elapsed, according to his estimate, before the copter touched ground again. The blindfold was taken off and Jules looked around, blinking at the harsh daylight after so long a period of darkness.

The copter was in the middle of a large open court-yard, with dirt underfoot. Around them were clumps of men going through various drilling exercises in groups of six or seven. A stone wall six meters high enclosed the yard on three sides, while on the fourth were a series of barracks-like buildings. *It's a regular army camp,* Jules thought, impressed. *They've certainly got organization, if nothing else.*

Jules' guards led him to the nearest of the buildings, which had a slightly more official look to it than the others. Inside, he was escorted to a small anteroom and told to wait. Two minutes later, he was ushered into the inner office.

The room was spartan in its simplicity. A battered wooden desk, a swivel chair, a table, two straight-backed wooden chairs and a chalkboard were the only furnishings. The window glasses had been partially opaqued to cut down on the glare from outside, and Jules—whose eyes had just gotten used to the brightness—now had to adjust to the lower level of lighting once again.

The man standing behing the desk had an impressive military bearing. He was one of the tallest Chandakhari Jules had ever seen, easily two meters tall, His posture was frighteningly erect, and his face bore the scars of countless street fights and melees. He was dressed in a simple brown caftan that went all the way to the floor.

"Welcome, Gospodin Koosman, to our little school." The man made no offer to shake hands, and instead pointed to a chair. Jules crossed the room and sat down; after he was seated, the other sat down as well. "My name is Jakherdi, and we will be getting to know each other quite well over the next few weeks."

"I'm sure I'll enjoy that, sir," Jules said politely.

The other man sneered. "I doubt that very much. I'm told that in your past experience you have killed men before. Is that correct?"

"Sure, it's hard to avoid it out on the streets."

"How many?"

"I never counted. Maybe a dozen, I don't know. There were two guards in the palace of the Baron of Calpuna, I do know that."

Jakherdi gave a small snort. "You'll have to become accustomed to perhaps three times that number in a week

126

if you work for us. And you will not kill them in a haphazard, streetfighter's style, either. Your kills will be neat, trim and businesslike. We will train you until it becomes routine, and you'll be working with others who've been as thoroughly trained as you. You will without emotion, for one motive only—profit. Killing out of passion weakens the soul, and we do not employ weak souls. Do I make myself clear?"

"Yes, very. But the police are looking for me. . . ."

"They won't be looking for you on Vesa, which is where we will take you when you've finished your training. Nor will they be looking for you here, since they don't know this place exists. Let us worry about the risks, Koosman; your sole concern is to learn what we teach and to perform well. If you do those two things, you will be rewarded far beyond your expectations. That's all I have to say to you now; someone will show you to your barracks and get you the supplies you'll need, then you'll join a novice training group. Good luck."

"Thank you, sir."

Jules was escorted to a building toward the back of the camp and assigned a bunk of his own. Since he had escaped from the prison without any belongings, he had no unpacking to do. Clothes were found that were approximately his size; he changed into them and was led outside to be introduced to the other new recruits.

That day was spent mostly in classroom activity. Jules received the basic indoctrination on what the group was like, what its motivation was and how it operated. He learned that victims were chosen at random by an advance member of the team who specialized in this kind of contact. This lead man would approach the victim or victims, strike up a casual conversation and determine whether they were worth killing. If they were, he would quickly work his way into their confidence and find some way of isolating them from everyone except his own people. They would be killed by strangulation, a team maneuver that made the victim helpless and made the kill most efficient. Their bodies would be stripped of valuables and then disposed of while one or two members of the team would go to the victim's hotel room and clean it out, leaving no trace. Return spaceship tickets were then cashed in, and the person ceased to be.

"There must be no doors left open behind us," the teacher emphasized. "This operation has lasted for twenty years because we carefully close off each possible lead to ourselves. There is no handle on us to grab. We are like the wind, sweeping what we can before us and then vanishing without trace."

"Excuse me, sir," Jules said, raising his hand. "May I be permitted a question?"

"You're here to learn, and questions help."

"You mentioned disposing of the bodies. If there are as many as you say, how can we dispose of them all without someone spotting them?" This had been the major puzzle he and Yvette had been unable to decipher. He hoped to get an answer now.

"Very intelligent point. We utilize the nature of Vesa itself. It is a closed, airless moon and has to recycle as much of its material as it can. Vesa had an admirably efficient recycling plant. We simply send the bodies there and they help maintain the balance of life on Vesa."

Once the explanation was given, the simplicity of it washed over Jules like a wave coming in to shore. Of course that was the answer! There would be no recognizable traces of the victims left, just a few centiliters of métallic wastes at the bottom of the recycling bin. Whoever had thought of this scheme had been thorough and brilliant in carrying it through.

After the classes they had a small lunch, then spent the rest of the afternoon out in the yard doing exercises and team drills, learning how to react to situations as a group and how to work together to achieve their objectives. The workout was easy to Jules, after the regimen he'd had to undergo as a circus performer, but it seemed grueling to his fellow students and so he pretended to be as tired as any of them when the day was through and they were fed their dinner. In the evening, there were classes in philosophy and meditation, to help them reach a state of peace within themselves so that the idea of mass murder would not seem so horrible. By 2200

128

hours, everyone was more than eager to get into bed and sleep.

Jules waited until he was sure everyone else in his barracks was asleep, then stole outside into the courtyard. He had to discover the location of this place if the Service was to make a clean sweep of the operation. Earlier in the day, while he'd been exercising, a breeze had wafted by, carrying with it a slight scent of the sea. He could hear no breakers, though, so he knew they must be some distance inland. The birds that perched on the wall were unfamiliar to him, but did not appear to have webbed feet; that wasn't much of an indication one way or another, though.

The night was clear, which was a blessing because he could see the stars. He had no instruments handy and no watch, so he could not even attempt to guess his longitude, but he could make a rough stab at latitude. He did not know the local constellations, but he could memorize the configurations of stars closest to the northern and southern horizons. When he was able to check some star charts at a later time, he'd be able to guess his approximate latitude—and with that information, plus the knowledge of the flying time in a copter from Bhangora, plus the knowledge that a seacoast was nearby, SOTE should be able to track down where this school was. It might take a little bit of effort, but the Service could muster a lot of resources if it needed them.

His observations completed, Jules started back to the barracks. He heard a noise and slipped into the deeper shadows as a sentry walked past. The man continued on his way without seeing anything and, as soon as he was gone, Jules returned to his bunk. With no indication that anything was amiss or that his absence had been noted, Jules slipped between the covers and went right to sleep.

The next day started as an exact copy of the one before. After a communal breakfast, Jules and his barracksmates were taken to a classroom and more instruction was begun on the philosophy of killing and the techniques the stranglers were to use. Films were shown depicting actual kills, with the instructor commenting on good and bad points of the killer's performances. To Jules, the idea of watching such a film was hideous, but he sat stony faced along with the others in the class and watched the action unfold before him.

Halfway through the film, though, there was an interruption as a messenger came into the room to tell the teacher that Jules was wanted in Jakherdi's office at once. Wondering what this obvious change in procedure could mean, Jules accompanied the messenger back to the administration building.

The secretary who had been in the outer office building yesterday was not there at present, leaving that room strangely quiet. Jules was instantly on guard against treachery. The messenger told Jules to go right into the inner office, that he was expected. *Maybe a little too expected*, Jules thought as he reached for the doorknob.

He opened the door, but made no immediate move to enter the room; instead, he looked around inside. Standing directly before him, silhouetted against the window, was Jakherdi, looking as impressively military as yesterday. On the desk in front of Jakherdi was a piece of paper that looked like a sketch of a face. Jules didn't need much intuition to tell him who the sketch represented.

They certainly work fast up on Vesa, he thought with a mental sigh. *Faster than I'd hoped.*

"Come in, Koosman," Jakherdi said crisply.

There were only two ways to go, forward or back. Even as he ticked off those options, Jules could feel the rear exit being closed. Some sixth sense told him of the presence of several people in the corridor outside the anteroom. Any attempt to go out that way would get him shot before he even reached the door.

Going into the office was the only alternative, and even that had to be a trap. Jules was sure the camp's superintendant would have at least one armed man on each side of the doorway out of view, just waiting for him to step inside. He didn't know whether the men had orders to stun or kill, but it made little difference; even if they only captured him now, they were certain to kill him later—after a shot of nitrobarb, more than likely.

He dared not hesitate. To do so was to reveal that he suspected the trap, in which case the gunmen would simply step out into view and shoot him instantly. He had no choice but to enter the trap; the method of entry, however, would be distinctly his own.

"Yes, sir," he answered aloud, taking the first step inside. "May I ask what the matter is?"

Then, before any more could be said, Jules acted. As his left foot came down from that first step, he bent it quickly under him and leaped forward. It was an off-balance leap and he wasn't able to get as much strength into it as he would have liked—but, coming as a surprise to the men inside the office, it was effective enough.

Jules landed just in front of the desk on his right leg, still off balance. He used that fact to advantage, spinning counterclockwise backwards on his right foot quickly off to the right side of the room. As he spun, he noticed that there were indeed two other men in the room, one on each side of the doorway, but they were caught flatfooted by his dramatic entrance. Before they could re-aim their weapons, Jules had braced his feet squarely, bent the knees and used his superpowerful leg muscles to propel him directly at the standing form of Jakherdi.

The camp master ducked, which was what Jules had been hoping he'd do. Curling himself into a ball, Jules tucked his head down and braced himself. His body hit the glass window like a hundred-kilo cannon ball. The shattering sound threatened to engulf the entire universe as Jules passed through the shards into the courtyard beyond.

There were a thousand little stings from the glass cuts, but they were mostly on his hands, the top of his head and the back of his neck—nonlethal places. His face and eyes had been securely tucked inside. He tumbled as he flew through the air toward the ground, but it was the controlled tumbling of a skilled aerialist. When he hit ground, he used the momentum of his flight to roll forward and spring to his feet, preparatory to running. A quick look around, however, was very discouraging.

The yard was filled with men, all armed with stunners.

They were surprised to see him come hurtling through the superintendent's window, but the time it took Jules to come to his feet gave them enough opportunity to overcome their surprise. They glared at him without emotion, but determination was written in their stances.

Even though he knew there was no chance against this number, Jules' spirit did not sag. *I can at least show them that a d'Alembert goes out fighting,* he thought, and charged at the nearest cluster of men.

A number five stunbeam lanced out and dropped him where he stood, and he fell to the ground in black oblivion.

Jakherdi looked out the hole in his window and gave a tight little smile upon seeing Jules' unconscious body. "Is he still alive?" he asked his men.

"Yes, sir. He'll be out for hours, though."

"Good. Tie him up securely. Remember, he's a Des-Plainian and can break out of ordinary ropes. Make sure he has barely enough room to breathe, then bring him in here to me. We have to ship him alive up to Vesa for questioning."

I pity you, Koosman or duChamps or whoever you are, the superintendent added silently to himself. *I know Garst and his methods. By the time he's finished with you you'll be begging him for death—only by that time it'll be far too late.*

CHAPTER 12

Secret Assaults

By the time she reached her hotel after her interview with the Marchioness, Yvette realized that there were several pairs of eyes watching her intently. Ignoring the stares, she strolled casually across the lobby and took the elevator tube down to her room. Garst had obviously decided to keep tabs on her, but it was a move she'd been expecting—she'd have done the same thing in his position.

She stayed in her room for half an hour, freshening up and making phone calls, then went out and spent the rest of the afternoon in innocuous activities like gambling and a sensable show. She took great pains to be obvious about what she was doing—she didn't want to lose those tails. At least, not yet.

In the early evening she returned to her hotel and ate a leisurely dinner in the dining room, then made no attempt to stifle a huge yawn as she descended the elevator tube to her room once more. It should be readily apparent to anyone watching that she was worn out and would be retiring for the night. Of course, that was not her intention at all.

Once safely inside the suite, there was no hint of fatigue as she set about her real purpose with determination. Forty-five minutes in front of a mirror with her makeup kit completely changed her face from that of the demure widow who had entered the room such a short while before. A long blonde wig in a carefully planned state of divine disarray added to her change in look. A skin-tight black leather jumpsuit—striking contrasted to the more moderate outfits worn by Carmen Velasquez—completed the disguise. Only the shrewdest of observers would recognize her as the same woman who had spent the day in such casual pursuits.

After a quick check to make sure she had all her equipment with her, she opened the door and walked out of her suite. One of the men Garst had assigned to follow her was seated on a bench by the elevator tubes at the end of the hallway. He looked up when her door opened and stared for a moment at her disguise, not believing it. Then his trained instincts came to the fore and he looked back at his newsroll, pretending not to notice.

Yvette sauntered up to him, noticing as she did so that there was no one else in the hallway at the moment. That would simplify things. As she reached into her bag, she said, "Good evening," then drew out Myerson's stunner and casually shot the man at point blank range before he could react. The number four stun would knock him out for at least two hours—plenty of time for her to get away without anyone being the wiser.

She took the up tube to the lobby and strolled through it. Every male eye in the place was on her as she swiveled her hips in sexy gyrations. Sometimes, she knew, the best disguise was to be blatant. The men who'd been assigned to follow her were watching, too, but they were seeing her as a sexual object, not as an assignment. She had an impish urge to walk directly up to one of them and wink at him broadly, but managed to resist the impluse. After all, there was no point in tempting fate.

Garst's men made no attempt to tail her as she left the lobby and hailed a jit on the street outside. They would have liked to, of course, but for entirely different reasons than before.

She had had no trouble earlier that day finding out where Garst lived; a few discreet phone calls from her room before she'd gone out gambling had gained her that information. She had checked the location on a map and formulated a plan of attack from that. Now she directed the driver of her jit to take her to the dome intersection that contained the entrance to Garst's house.

The more she thought about it, the more convinced she was that Garst had to be the man behind this whole conspiracy. It had been obvious from the meeting this afternoon that he could wrap the Marchioness around his little finger and make her do anything he wanted. He had the intelligence, the cunning and the coldness to set up an organization like this and keep it running for two decades without detection.

As one of the top agents for the Service of the Empire, it was well within her authority to declare him a traitor just on the basis of what she already knew and execute him on the spot. Without his genius for organization, the conspiracy he had fostered so carefully would struggle along and eventually break up into small cliques that could be dealt with more efficiently by local agencies. Her assignment would be considered accomplished and no one, not even the Head himself, would be able to criticize her handling of the affair.

But that was not the way Yvette d'Alembert liked to

work. She was well aware of the responsibility that went with her authority over matters of life and death. She had to have irrefutable proof that Garst was indeed behind this before she would act—and it was to obtain such proof that she was now paying a visit to his house. Besides, she was hoping to get enough information to crack the whole gang wide open immediately, rather than waiting for it to fall apart on its own after Garst's demise.

The jit reached her destination and Yvette got off and surveyed the area. The job would be a little harder than she'd anticipated, as she realized that breaking and entering was a much more hazardous occupation on Vesa than anywhere else in the Empire. Nearly all houses were built underground, below street level, meaning that there were no windows or upper stories to enter through. Also, being an underground settlement, the lights were kept on round the clock, making it most difficult to skulk about in shadows.

The only way to break in, Yvette decided, would be to confront the problem directly. The hour she had chosen for her break-in was technically nighttime, though that meant little on Vesa. People could be—and were—awake at all hours, but she was hoping that Garst would not be at home. Walking boldly up to the door, she tried pushing down the latch. It would not move, indicating the door was locked. That usually meant either no one was home or the occupants were asleep, and that was an encouraging sign.

Reaching into her purse, Yvette pulled out a small passkey kit. The door lock was a standard one that could be opened by the right combination of electronic impulses. The passkey device she held was an extremely intricate and expensive piece of equipment. An ultraminiature computer, it systematically ran through billions of possible combinations in a matter of seconds, making an almost untamperable lock passable. In less than a minute, Yvette heard the click informing her that the lock mechanism had been turned off and the door could be opened.

She replaced the passkey in her purse and removed now the current detector. Far and away the most common burglar alarm in use was one that would go off if an electrical

135

circuit were broken——by, for instance, opening the door while the alarm was turned on. Sure enough, a quick check with her sensor revealed that Garst's door was wired with just such a system. The detector allowed Yvette to trace the circuit around the door frame; then, with a pinpoint laser drill, she bored through the wooden frame at specific sites and was able to jump the system with some cables she had brought herself. Then, after another check to make sure there were no other alarms attached, she quietly opened the door and slipped inside.

The interior of the house was dark, but Yvette had come prepared for that eventuality. She slipped on a pair of specially treated goggles and pulled a small infrared flashlight out of her purse. The glow it gave the house was an eerie one, but it was good enough for Yvette to see by without alarming anyone who might be inside. Thus equipped, she set off to explore Garst's mansion.

The long hallway contained just a few chairs, a small table and a clock hanging on the wall. The closet was just that, a place to hang cloaks and hats; she rapped lightly on the walls, floor and ceiling, but could detect no hiding places within it.

She moved on to the first room, which was a living room. Yvette noticed that Garst had top-quality furniture, better than the Marchioness's though less flashy; obviously, he was a man of some taste. There were a lot of places for her to check, particularly two rows of bookcases against the far wall, but she went through them with the efficiency of the professional that she was. The next room, the dining room, was more sparsely furnished, and it too checked out clean.

One door led out of the dining room to what she presumed would be the kitchen; another, smaller door stood on the other side locked and defiant. A quick check showed her that the room was locked mechanically rather than electronically, but that there were no alarms attached to the door. Using her laser drill in a slightly different fashion, she quickly burned out the lock mechanism and opened the door.

She found herself in a room that was smaller than either the living room or dining room. It appeared to be a study of some sort, probably very comfortable but at the same time there was something about it that seemed menacing. A small wooden desk stood in one corner, its top littered with papers and bookreels. The residue receptacle was crammed with the butts of stale cigarettes and dopesticks.

Yvette went quickly over and examined some of the papers. The writing did not show up very well under her infrared light, but it did seem to be strings of numbers. Of course, it was only natural that the Marchioness's First Advisor would be doing paperwork involving figures, but Yvette wondered whether these numbers might not represent other interests as well. Taking her minicam out of her purse, she proceeded to photograph the pages so that they could be studied in more detail at her leisure.

When she'd finished with the papers on the top of the desk she tried the drawers to see what she would discover in there. The drawers were locked, but she was able to force them open with nothing more elaborate than her pocketknife. There seemed to be the usual office supplies and stationery in most of the drawers, but in the bottom one she detected a false backing. Prying it out, she discovered a set of bookreels. *I wonder why he's hiding these. Could they contain the records for his criminal organization?*

Her sharp ears detected a slight sound behind her and she whirled around, her hand simultaneously reaching into her purse for Myerson's stunner. But at that same instant the lights in the room were switched on abruptly, blinding her through the goggles with their sudden intensity. Blinking back tears, she strained to see who had surprised her.

"Easy, gospozha," came a cool voice. "There are four guns trained on you this instant. I'd suggest you take your hands out of the purse *very* slowly."

As her eyes rapidly adjusted to the light she could make out that the speaker was not Garst, but a short, stubby man. He had spoken the truth, though; behind him were three other men, and all of them were armed with stunners.

Yvette did as the man suggested, looking for the precise moment when their guards would relax enough for her to make her move. The one thing that was working in her favor was that they probably would not be expecting a woman to be as fast and tough as she was.

When he could see that her hand was empty of weapons, the man relaxed a bit. "That's better. Now, toss your purse over in the corner there." Again, Yvette complied. "Garst was expecting something on this order, and when we found you'd slipped our noose back at your hotel we came straight here." He stepped to within a meter of her, the muzzle of his gun dropping ever so slightly. "Please hand over that bookreel, if you don't mind."

In a casual gesture, Yvette raised her left hand to brush the long blonde hair of her wig out of her eyes. The wig was held onto her head by a special glue that would come off at a sharp tug without pulling her real hair with it. "Since you asked so politely, all right," she said evenly, picking the bookreel up off the desktop with her right hand and extending it toward the leader of her captors.

As he reached out to take it from her, Yvette acted. Whipping the wig off her head with the left hand, she flung it directly into the man's face. Her captor instinctively lifted both arms to protect his eyes from the flying object and Yvette took advantage of the opening. Lunging forward, she drove her powerful right fist—still clutching the reel—into his solar plexus. The man gave a dismal *whoosh*, dropped his gun and fell to the floor doubled over with the pain. He would be in no condition to oppose her for several minutes at least.

There were three other armed men to contend with; but Yvette was in motion while they were starting from a standstill. All three had been backed up against the wall behind their leader, which left them little room to maneuver. Yvette swung around to their sides, so that only the first of them would have a chance to shoot her; his body would block the shots of the other two.

In a movement so fast it looked like a streak, Yvette slapped the gun out of his hand. The stunner crashed against the wall and then fell to the ground. Long before it reached the floor under the slow pull of Vesa's gravity, however, Yvette had brought up her right foot and kicked the gunman squarely in the gut. The man fell backwards into his two companions, and the trio toppled groundward.

Yvette recovered her balance from the kick and dived after them. She landed on top of the unholy heap, grabbed each of the men in turn by his hair and banged his skull hard against the floor. All three were out cold and the fight was over within fifteen seconds of her first move with the wig.

Going over to the stumpy man who'd done all the talking, she picked up his stunner and sat waiting, poised on the edge of Garst's desk with the muzzle pointed directly at him. He choked and gasped for several minutes; when she felt he was ready to converse again she nudged him with the toe of her boot. "Where's Garst?"

The man shook his head. "Don't . . . don't know."

"He is the head of this murderer's guild of yours, isn't he?"

"Y-yes, but . . . out. He's out."

Yvette grimaced. She had the confirmation she wanted, but not the man. "Where's his appointment calendar?"

"Top drawer."

Yvette found what she was looking for quickly and checked today's date. According to his schedule, Garst was supposed to be meeting now with Marchioness Gindri at her palace. "Thanks for the help," she said, then squeezed the trigger stud on the stunner. The man collapsed from the number four bolt, and Yvette knew he'd be safely unconscious for at least a couple of hours.

Moving over to the desk phone, she put in a call to the private number she'd been given for Marask Kantana. When the SOTE chief answered, Yvette identified herself quickly and told her to get every available agent she could up to Vesa immediately. She was to dispatch one person to Garst's mansion to pick up the four men who would be waiting there unconscious; the rest were to meet her at the Marchioness's palace.

Kantana nodded assent. When agent Periwinkle gave an order, any SOTE chief who valued her job would obey without question. She informed Yvette that it would take two hours to get from Chandakha, where she was based, up to Vesa, but that she would be there in not one second more. Yvette accepted the explanation and signed off. She still had some work to do.

After seeing to it that all four of her would-be captors received stuns that would keep them here until the next SOTE agent arrived to arrest them, Yvette retrieved her purse from the corner where she'd tossed it and, making no pretense at silence or caution, raced out of the house to the street. Hailing a jit after two minutes, she directed it to the Marchioness's palace. The driver was startled by Yvette's appearance—after all, one did not normally visit the Marchioness at this hour in a black leather jumpsuit and disheveled hair—but offered no objections when Yvette gave her a twenty-ruble tip to hurry.

The time for all pussyfooting was over, a fact that made Yvette feel very, very good. The surges of adrenalin through her body were being matched by feelings of vengeance as she conjured up a mental image of Dak's handsome face. *Now I'll get them for you, Dak,* she thought as the jit rolled along through the tunnels of Vesa. Her hands clenched in anticipation.

When the shuttle arrived at the palace, Yvette leaped out and ran up to the massive front gates. There was a doorman on either side, but Yvette did not have the time to determine whether they were just honest servants or possible spies in the employ of Garst; to make sure, she gave them each a number four jolt from her stunner. She had made sure Myerson's gun was fully charged before she left her hotel room, meaning that she still had nearly fifty shots left. There wouldn't be nearly that many staff on duty tonight, which meant she could take out everyone inside. She blessed the fact that the stun-gun was such a humane weapon—she could use it indiscriminately, without having to make instant decisions about guilt or innocence, and there would be no permanent after-effects if her move was wrong.

She passed through the gates without stopping and moved into the palace itself. Racing down the long, cold hallways she shot at everyone she met with pinpoint accuracy, leaving a trail of unconscious bodies in her wake.

She stormed through every room in the enormous palace, clearing it of potential foes, until at last she came to the Marchioness's boudoir.

The hereditary ruler of Vesa was lying in her enormous plush bed eating what must have been for her a light snack—a small capon, a plate of vegetables and a goblet of white wine. So quickly and quietly had Yvette moved through the palace that the Marchioness had had no warning of this invasion. She looked up, startled, then belatedly recognized Yvette as the woman she'd spoken to earlier that day. "You!" she exclaimed. "What are you doing here? What gave you the audacity. . . ?"

Yvette at first had ignored the fat woman. This was the last room of the palace, and as yet she had seen no sign of Garst. Her eyes quickly swept the room, but there was no trace of the First Advisor here, either. She turned to the Marchioness Gindri, gun pointed, and cut off the diatribe. "Where's Garst?" she demanded.

The Marchioness was quite flustered to have a weapon aimed at her. Nothing like that had ever happened before. "Why should I tell you?"

"Because if you don't I'll give you a shot of nitrobarb that could kill you, and you'll tell me anyhow. There's no use calling for help, I've neutralized everyone in the palace. It's just you and me." She gestured menacingly with the stunner. "Now talk."

"He . . . he was here until just a little while ago," Gindri stammered nervously. "Then he got a call and he left."

"What was the call about?"

"I don't . . . don't know, exactly. Something about a DesPlainian spy being caught or something. He had to go question him."

Yvette's heart skipped a beat. That "DesPlainian spy" could only be Jules! She had seen his message in the newsroll a week ago that he was going down to Chandakha; when had he returned, and how had he been captured? She had to know. Grabbing the fat, ugly woman by the shoulders and digging her fingers deeply into the mealy flesh, she said, "Where did he go to meet them?"

"I don't . . . wait, I think he said something about the

recycling plant. That way, they wouldn't have far to go to get rid of the body afterwards, he said."

"How long ago was that?"

"Fifteen, maybe twenty minutes."

There may still be time, Yvette thought. Looking at her watch, she saw that it would be more than an hour yet before Kantana arrived with her people. *I can't wait that long,* she decided. *Jules' life may be at stake.*

Aloud, she said, "Thanks for your help, even if it was involuntary." Then she gave the Marchioness a number four stun, the same as everyone else.

Taking a stylus and pad from her purse, she quickly encoded a message explaining the situation and where to meet her, then posted the note where Kantana could not miss it as she entered the palace.

I only hope I won't be too late, she thought as she waited impatiently for a jit to come by that she could commandeer to take her to the recycling plant.

CHAPTER 13

The Battle of the Recycling Plant

Consciousness returned slowly to Jules. The first thing he was definitely aware of was a constriction in his chest, a difficulty in breathing. By reflex he began gasping, but there was something preventing him from expanding his chest as far as he needed for comfort. The inside of his mouth was exceedingly dry, as though it had been washed out with desert sand. His throat was sore, and swallowing was difficult. He winced involuntarily as he tried gulping the small amount of saliva his glands had produced.

He felt light-headed and dizzy. In fact, his entire body felt light, as though he were floating in a sea of jelly. As his consciousness drifted in and out, he realized slowly that he must be either out in space or back on Vesa, where the gravity was far less than on Chandakha. But for the moment the fact was only of academic interest;

142

his mind was still too fuzzed over to care about such things.

He tried to open his eyes, but the lids felt glued together. There was light around him, though; he could tell from the redness penetrating the membranes. There were sounds around him, too, voices drifting in and out of some auditory fog, but individual words utterly failed to register on his brain. He floated in this state of apathy for an indeterminate time, not caring what happened to him.

He was jolted out of the dreamy state by a hand slapping him hard across the right cheek. The shock was enough to open his eyes and stir up the thought processes in his brain once more. His vision was blurred and doubled, and it took all the power of his still-numbed mind to concentrate and focus on his surroundings.

Standing before him was a lanky man whom he belatedly recognized as the man who'd been lecturing at the warehouse the night he'd spied on them. Behind him were two dozen other men, equally threatening. There was a tight grin of vengeance on the man's face as he stared down at Jules, who found that he was seated on a chair, bound tightly hand and foot. "Well," the man's voice boomed in Jules' ears, "so you've finally come out of it, have you?"

Jules was still too dazed to reply. His tongue lay like a lump of lead in his mouth, refusing to move. As the fog began to lift from his senses, he became aware of the foul odor in the air. It seemed a mixture of every disgusting smell known to man, from the aroma of fecal matter through the stench of decaying meat. Jules tried closing his nostrils, an impossible feat, and finally had to settle for breathing through his mouth as much as possible.

The man stood over Jules and slapped him again, this time with the other hand. He hit with such force that it literally made Jules' teeth rattle inside his mouth. Jules found his temper rising and had to force himself to keep it under control. "It's not for nothing that the phrase 'losing your head' is equivalent to 'losing your temper'," he remembered his father telling him. A man blinded by rage could miss an opportunity that a calmer man would spot. *I should be thankful he's hitting me,* Jules thought. *He's bringing me out of the stupor a lot faster, and that's to my advantage.*

He tried to maintain the glazed look on his face a little while longer, though, as he stared about the rest of the room. It was big, easily one of the largest chambers he'd ever seen. The ceiling was literally covered with pipes of various diameters, some of which went out through holes in the wall to other rooms, and others of which were connected to the enormous vats that stood like giant sentinels scattered about the floor. The smallest of the vats was easily five meters tall and eight meters in diameter, and there were others that absolutely dwarfed it in size. Metal ladders ran up and down the lengths of these vats, and catwalks encircled the tops. And everywhere was the disgusting stench of death and decay.

"You've got a lot to answer for, you know," the man in front of Jules said, forcing the DesPlainian to return his attention to immediate concerns. "We've had to waste a lot of our time and energy trying to find you. We didn't like that."

Jules' tongue was feeling less fuzzy now, and he could attempt to talk. "If I'd known," he slurred, "I'd have left my business card."

His inquisitor hit him again, but this time Jules was expecting it and was able to turn his head with the blow to minimize its effect. "Insolence will not be excused," the man said harshly. "I will give you your due, however. You fought quite well. And no one has ever been able to infiltrate our training camp before. You must have had help—very highly placed help."

Jules had to get his questioner off that train of thought. If that idea were followed to its logical conclusion, it would be obvious that Jules was working for SOTE. Only the Service of the Empire would have been able to concoct his phony prison record, get him into the prison and help him bust out so convincingly. And if these crooks ever got even the faintest suspicion that SOTE was on to them, they'd vanish into the night and the Service would never be able to track them all down. Not to mention

144

the fact that Jules would be dead the instant after they came to that realization.

To forestall the man's thinking the problem out to the inevitable conclusion, Jules said, "Nah, it wasn't any problem at all. Your people'd take a cross-eyed nangabat if it flew in and asked for a job."

The man raised his arm to strike once more, then stopped. "No, I think there's been enough of that for now," he decided. "We'll have to think of some other way to entertain you. . . ."

There was a knocking at the door to one side. "Get that," the man called to some of the other men in the room. Then, thinking better of it, he said, "No, I'll get it. It's probably Garst."

As he walked away, the eyes of the others all went with him. All, that is, except for those of one young man who silently detached himself from a group of his fellows and edged between the vats to stand beside Jules. The SOTE agent recognized the lad as Radapur, the Chandakhar he'd saved from Rask's mad attack out on the spaceport field.

No one else in the room saw Radapur approach or stand beside him. The youth had a sharp knife clutched firmly in his hand. There was an expression on the lad's face that was impossible for Jules to fathom, so twisted was it with conflicting emotions. *Is he coming to kill me or free me?* he wondered.

Radapur was behind him now and, with several quick slashes, cut the bonds that held Jules in place. "The debt is paid," the youth said tersely. "I can do no more." And he moved away again so quickly that Jules would hardly have believed he'd ever been there, were it not for the slashed ropes behind him.

He had no chance to make any break now, however, as the door opened and closed quickly and attention was turning back in his direction. The ropes were hanging more slackly on him, and Jules hoped fervently that no one would notice until he had an opportunity to make his move.

"Whew," said the newcomer, "I'd forgotten the stench

of this place. I'm glad I don't have to come down here much anymore. Where's the spy?"

"Over this way." The tall man led the newcomer over to where Jules was seated. It was obvious from the deference in his attitude that the late arrival was a man of importance in this organization—perhaps the big boss himself. Jules stared at the face, but the man was no one he had met. There was a craftiness to that face, though, and an evil glint behind the eyes.

As Jules was studying his face, the boss—Garst, he had been called—was studying Jules. "DesPlainian, all right," he mused aloud. "The skin's dyed of course, now, but even so . . . there's more than a superficial resemblance to that girl."

Yvette! Had she already tangled with this man? If so, what had happened? Why was he still free to walk around, and what had become of his sister? Those questions and a thousand others flooded Jules' mind. It was only with a great force of will that he put them aside and concentrated on his position of the moment. He could worry about Yvette sometime later, when he was less worried about himself.

Garst gave him no more clues. Instead, he turned to his lieutenant and asked, "All right, Lessin, what have you learned from him so far?"

"Nothing yet. He's only just come out of stun. I wanted to wait until you got here before giving him the juice. You would know better what questions to ask him."

Garst nodded. "Okay, get on with it."

Lessin reached into a leather pouch at his belt and pulled out a hyposprayer filled with a clear fluid. The "juice," as he had called it, could only be nitrobarb, which would knock its victim into a coma for twenty minutes, after which he would have to answer any and all questions put to him. For Jules, it would be the death knell; even if the drug itself did not kill him, Garst and his men were certain to once they learned what he knew. His life was on the line, and he'd have to make his move now.

As Lessin approached him with the sprayer, Jules suddenly lifted one leg and kicked the strangler squarely amidship. The man let out a grunt of surprise and pain, and fell backwards. The hyposprayer flew from his hand and landed across the room, shattering on impact with the floor and spilling its lethal contents harmlessly on the concrete surface.

Long before that happened, however, the rest of the room had exploded into action. Garst, his reflexes faster than Jules would have given him credit for, backed away from the DesPlainian the instant his foot lashed out at Lessin, and began reaching for the gun he had tucked away in his jacket pocket. The rest of the gang, two dozen of them, were all armed as well—they'd seen Jules in action before and had come prepared for anything. Even Radapur was reaching for his gun. Apparently the young man felt that cutting the bonds and giving Jules a chance to fight for his freedom was ample enough repayment; from now on it would be no quarter asked or given. Jules accepted that as an unhappy fact of life and planned accordingly.

He had been hoping to grab Garst and hold him in front as a hostage to ensure safe passage out of here, but the man had jumped out of reach too quickly for him to accomplish that. Besides, with a group like this there was always the possibility of one of the lesser murderers taking it into his head to shoot the boss as well and take over for himself. While in the long run that might lead to the group's unity dissolving in internal rivalries, in the short run it would do Jules no good whatsoever.

The SOTE agent sized up the situation quickly. All his opponents were armed; while some of the weapons they had were stunners, most were equipped with bigger stuff —blasters, and heavy-duty ones at that. This game was being played for keeps, and Jules could afford no mistakes. One slip here and he was dead.

Getting quickly to his feet Jules bounded abruptly in the direction opposite to Garst. The long high leap left him in a vulnerable position momentarily as it took several seconds for Vesa's light gravity to pull him back to the ground again; but his aerialist training came to his assistance once more as he curled himself into a small ball and spun through the air, offering a minimal target surface for the killers to aim at. He felt the scorching heat as several bolts passed by within half a meter of him, but fortunately these killers were used to strangling their victims and were not as adept with guns as they might be.

Jules had gauged his leap to take him behind one of the nearby vats. He straightened out as he approached ground level, noticing as he did so that there were no more bolts going past his immediate vicinity. He was out of direct, straight-line range, and therefore safe—for the moment.

"Watch those blasters in here!" Garst called out. "We can't afford to damage anything, or we might all be flooded out. Stunners only, unless you've got an absolutely clear shot. Don't move too quickly, don't overcommit yourself. Remember, there's only one way out and we're guarding it. He's trapped in here and we outnumber him, so it's only a matter of time."

Garst is right, Jules grimaced. As long as he was weaponless and there were armed men at the door his chances of escape were virtually nil. He could bounce around for hours, gradually wearing himself out, while they could move at their leisure and hunt him down. Getting possession of a weapon of his own would be a big help, but in the meantime he would have to stay in motion and avoid letting the enemy get any clear shots at him.

As he touched ground he jumped again, this time for the ladder that went up the side of the vat next to him. Using the handrails he pulled himself up five rungs at a time until he was almost to the top. The sounds of running footsteps told him that his pursuers were coming around after him, closing in on the spot where he'd disappeared from their view. Turning around and bracing himself against the ladder, he leaped through the air towards the top of the next vat some five meters away. Again, his leap seemed agonizingly slow to him as Vesa's low gravity worked lazily to pull him down. One of the men below him spotted him during his leap and fired a blaster bolt up at him, but it passed harmlessly a meter away as Jules finally came down on the catwalk around the rim of the vat he'd aimed for.

As he landed, the forward momentum of his leap almost carried him headfirst into the vat, but he managed to grab the railing and stop his motion. As he was leaning over the vat, though, he got a good strong whiff of its contents—hundreds of thousands of liters of human waste products. Though efforts had been taken to neutralize the odor they were never a hundred percent successful. The fumes were so overpowering that Jules sank to his knees, gagging and retching. *This is obviously the recycling plant,* he thought as he knelt there helplessly for a moment. *And if I don't want to get recycled myself, I'd better get moving again.*

Still choking, he pulled himself to his feet and raced around the perimeter of the vat. Shots were fired up at him, but none of them came close. One shot did hit one of the overhead pipes, however, burning a hole in it and showering the entire area with a steamy, salted liquid. Keeping his head bowed down so that none of the fluid would get in his eyes, Jules continued running. Below him, he heard Garst chewing out his men and telling them to be more careful about how they shot.

From his lofty vantage point, Jules could see one man off to one side, separated from the rest of his fellows and out of their sight. With an outward leap, Jules plunged off the catwalk toward the ground, falling much faster than the normal gravity would allow because he had given himself a push in the right direction. In midair he twisted his body around like a cat so that he was falling feet first. A fall from such a height under Earth gravity could be fatal to an untrained person, and even on Vesa it could have serious consequences, but Jules knew precisely what he was doing.

His feet hit the lone gangster squarely in the chest just under the chin. The man crumpled to the floor with his ribs caved in, but his body broke Jules' fall and cushioned the landing impact. The DesPlainian rolled to his feet, grabbed the man's gun—only a stunner, unfortunately—and began running. He reached another vat and began climbing the ladder, making it halfway up before he was spotted again. The man who saw him gave cry, but it was the last thing he ever did; Jules mowed him down with one perfectly placed shot, and his stunner was set on ten—instantly lethal.

He made it to the top of the vat and looked around. The contents of this tank was garbage of various sorts, but the odor was no more pleasant than the last one. From this spot, though, Jules could get a clear look at the door and the two men standing guard in front of it. Since they weren't part of the chase, they had no definite idea as to where he was. Their eyes scanned the room nervously, waiting for him to make a break in their direction so that they could gun him down.

Two quick shots were all Jules needed to fell that pair in their tracks. He had hoped that, in the excitement, no one would notice that he had gotten them and he would be able to slip out the door. But Garst's sharp eyes spotted their deaths immediately. Barking crisp orders, the leader of the murderers sent another pair of his men to guard the egress, but this time he told them not to stand immediately in front of the door unprotected. Instead, he had them take up positions behind the vats with their guns trained on the door. Anyone trying to get out would be instantly killed in the crossfire.

A blaster bolt struck the handrail just centimeters from Jules' hand, turning the rail to molten slag in that spot and making it too hot for Jules to hold onto. He backed away and aimed a fast shot at the man who'd fired at him, but the other had ducked back under cover too quickly.

There are just too many of them, Jules thought as he recovered his breath and prepared to move to a new perch. *I can't keep hopping around like this indefinitely. Sooner or later, one of them's bound to get lucky and hit me.* But he knew there was no choice—he had to try.

Just as he was preparing for another leap, though, the doors to the plant burst open inward and Yvette raced in, stunner in hand. She stopped for a moment to evaluate the wild scene before her, and everyone else stopped as well, startled by this unexpected development. The guards watching the door also hesitated; they were expecting to shoot someone trying to get out, not trying to get in, and they were undecided what to do. Their indecision would only last a second, though, and Yvette was a sitting duck in her exposed position unless she could be warned.

The age-old circus danger call of "Hey, Rube!" had survived through the centuries, albeit in an abbreviated form. So Jules' cry of "Rube!" evoked an instant response from his sister. She dived forward, low to the ground, just as two blaster bolts criss-crossed through the space where her head had been a split second earlier. She hit the deck, rolled, and came up ready for action.

Yvette's sudden appearance made Jules feel reborn. The odds of twenty to one had seemed almost hopeless, but now they were down to ten to one. Why, that was practically child's play!

With renewed spirits, he suddenly changed role from hunted to hunter. Each opponent he could pick off would reduce the odds that much more, and each of the men on the ground knew that they no longer had only one quarry to contend with. They had to watch from all angles at once, lest they be picked off by Jules' new ally. They sensed immediately a change in the atmosphere, and switched to a defensive posture.

Yvette was a hurricane on legs as she raced about the vast chamber in a cold fury. She seemed to have no fear at all as she ran at top speed between the vats, sometimes straight at groups of the killers. At one point she felled four of the men in half as many seconds by coming on them by surprise, before they had a chance to react. She was driving the stranglers frantic with her relentless assaults on their positions—and if any of them was careless enough to move too quickly out of her way, Jules was usually perched right above to pick him off from that direction. Steadily the number of opponents dwindled until, after only a couple of minutes, it was they who were on the defensive totally, just trying to stay live between this Scylla and Charybdis of DesPlainian fury.

Jules had never seen his sister so worked up, so absolutely coldblooded about her business. She took risks—some of them quite unnecessary, in his opinion—as though she had no fear of death. *She's a demon today*, he thought as he watched her flit like a black shadow across the floor. *I wonder what's gotten into her*. But he was kept too busy shooting at the murderers to spend much time thinking about it. He recovered his breath and his strength as he concentrated on his target practice.

Soon the number of the enemy had been whittled down until only Garst was left alone. He had taken to hiding at the far corner of the room, protected by machinery on several sides. But now, with the attention of both DesPlainians focused solely on him, he knew he would never be able to hold out. In desperation he bolted from the spot, running along the back wall of the plant in an effort to reach the door before the two SOTE agents could get to him.

Jules found he was entirely out of position to try to capture Garst, and the crime boss was out of stunner range. Instead, the DesPlainian started leaping from vat to vat, working his way across the room in an attempt to reach the door before Garst could. Yvette, who was already down on the floor, would have a better chance of confronting Garst directly.

Garst had a good lead on her, but Yvette was moving at superhuman speed at the moment and closed the gap between them rapidly. Stopping in front of a large opened door marked "Chemical Reprocessing," the First Advisor took careful aim with his blaster and directed a bolt straight at Yvette. The female d'Alembert made a minute swerve and the deadly beam touched ground only centimeters from her feet, scorching the concrete flooring. Yvette didn't even slow down.

A look of terror now crossed the face of the man whose organization had so callously doomed hundreds of thousands of people to death. This was more a machine than a person coming at him, a black-clad juggernaut bent solely on his destruction. He tried to start running again, but his foot slipped on the ground that was now covered by the liquid spewing from the leaking pipe above. He spread out his arms to regain his balance, but to no avail. With a cry of doomed anguish he fell through the opened door and disappeared from view.

As she came to the wet spot, Yvette slowed her own charge so that she wouldn't suffer the same fate. Walking carefully up to the edge of the door, she peered inside.

Below her, surrounded by a narrow walkway, steamed a vat of chemicals whose purpose was to reduce organic materials to their basic molecular components. These components would then be filtered out into separate tanks and recombined in more acceptable form for human consumption. There was no chance that any living thing could fall in there and survive.

As she stared into the greenish liquid her hands clenched and unclenched several times in frustration. She had wanted to take Garst apart personally, piece by piece, but consoled herself with the thought that his death had not been a particularly pleasant one. She found that her lower jaw was trembling, and stopped it with an act of will. "He's gone," she announced simply.

Her brother came racing up to her and put his arms around her. Suddenly all the tensions of the last two days hit Yvette at once and she leaned, trembling, in his embrace. Jules held her tightly and said nothing. He wanted very much to ask her what the matter was, but he knew his sister too well for that. He didn't want to hurt her pride. When she was ready to tell him the story, she would do so. In the meantime he would offer her all the aid he could without invading her privacy.

After a couple of minutes Yvette pulled herself together and smiled up at her brother. "This affected me a little more strongly than I thought."

He nodded. "You know, I've discovered I don't like working on my own nearly as well. It gets awfully lonely sometimes."

"Yes." She continued to smile weakly, then looked down at her feet. "Yes, it does." After a moment she looked back up at him, her face back to its normal composure. "Chief Kantana and her agents should be arriving soon at the Marchioness's palace. I asked them to meet me there, since that was where I thought Garst would be. Gindri was in collusion with Garst, but he was the brains. As soon as I learned he would be here, I left a note for them to follow me." She looked around at the devastation the evening's activities had wrought at the plant. "There's nothing really for them to do here. Why

153

don't you go back to the palace and help them sort out the pieces there?"

"What about you?"

"I'll be along in a little bit. I just have a private goodbye to say here, that's all. Don't worry, I'll be all right."

Jules gave her a quizzical glance, but said nothing. As he walked out the door, he turned to look back. Yvette was standing beside the opening to the chemical processing vat, staring blankly into it. There were tears in her eyes, though whether they were from the chemical fumes or some inner grief he could not tell. With a shrug of the shoulders, Jules turned and left his sister to work out her emotions for herself.

CHAPTER 14

The Chandakha Solution

They sent a coded report directly to the Head the next day, and received an answer within two hours. They were ordered to return on the next available ship, and to leave the mopping-up operations in the capable hands of Chief Kantana. They were both a little sorry not to be able to finish completely what they'd started, but they realized the wisdom of their superior's decision. After all, they were his top agents and their talents shouldn't be wasted on trivia. There were plenty of other people to handle the routine work.

Despite their own impatience, the Head suggested that they take their time getting back. The ship on which they booked passage took a leisurely ten days to make the trip to Earth—time they used well for both emotional and physical healing. Yvette told her brother all about Dak and her feelings for him, and he comforted her to the best of his ability. By the time they reached Earth, Yvette was reconciled to Dak's death. He was only a dull ache in the back of her mind—if not forgotten, at least put aside for other matters.

154

They came down at the Canaveral Spaceport in Florida and drove in their own jet-car to the Hall of State building for Sector Four, located in Miami. Landing on the rooftop, they took the private elevator tube down to the Head's office, where Duchess Helena showed them in with great ceremony.

Grand Duke Zander von Wilmenhorst was seated behind his large desk which was, as usual, buried beneath a mass of paperwork. He looked much more at home in these surroundings than he did in his spaceship; the milieu was suited to his basic personality. He waved them casually into chairs and Helena went automatically to the bar. Knowing the d'Alemberts' preference for nonalcoholic beverages, she fixed them both orange juice freezes.

"Once again I have to commend you two on a superlative job," he said when everyone had gotten comfortably settled. "It threatens to become a habit. Of course it's a pleasant habit to acquire, considering the alternatives.

"You're no doubt wondering how the mop-up operations went. I got a report in just yesterday from Kantana, and her work has been perfect. The ledger reel you found, Yvette, did indeed contain some of Garst's records, as well as some notes that let Kantana discover where he'd hidden the rest of his files. They went right back to the beginning of his organization, more than two decades ago. The wealth that flowed through that group was greater than the Gross Planetary Products of many smaller worlds! It was an incredible system. Garst was an organizational genius, and I'm glad he's dead. I'd hate to know he's still out there plotting. It was only an accident that led us to him at all.

"So many criminals slip up by getting too greedy, but Garst kept a tight rein on that. He preyed on only small numbers of tourists—comparatively, of course—where a lesser man might have tried for bigger scores. By keeping at a low level continuously, he was able to get away with his crimes far longer than he should have."

The Head absently shifted papers from one stack to another as he spoke. "Once we had the records, of course, it was a simple matter for Kantana to round up all the members of the gang on Vesa, including the corrupt police and hotel and recycling plant employees. And from the information you gave her, Jules, she was able to track down their training school. There wasn't much left of it—Jakherdi had burned it down and scattered his personnel the moment word reached him about Garst's death—but Garst's records were complete enough that she knew who she was looking for. A few of the small fry have escaped detection in Chandakha's crowds, but all the major officers in the conspiracy have been captured."

Shifting uneasily in his chair, Jules sipped at his drink and looked thoughtful. When he was certain that his boss had finished speaking for the moment, he began, "On the way back to Earth I did a bit of thinking. We've smashed the conspiracy on Vesa for now, but I really don't think we've solved the problem."

The Head raised an eyebrow speculatively. "Oh? How do you mean?"

"Well, the real menace is Chandakha. Garst could never have set up the system he did if he didn't have a steady supply of people to commit his murders. He needed hundreds of men who were so desperate for money and so calloused about the value of human life that they could kill automatically, like machines. Chandakha is a breeding ground for exactly that sort of person. Life is the cheapest commodity they have there. People are so crammed together, crime is so rampant, that recruiting for a strangler's guild is simplicity itself. Transport a man from the slums of Bhangora to the flashy casinos of Vesa and he's bound to feel resentment against the rich. Why shouldn't he take what they have if he can? They have more than enough, and his family is starving."

The Head nodded gravely. "Everything you're saying is right. What do you propose be done about it?"

"The people have to be dispersed," Jules said with determination. "They can't go on living jammed together like that. Garst was actually providing Chandakha with a safety valve, though I doubt whether he thought of it in those terms. By perpetually bleeding off the worst members of Chandakha's society, he kept the planet from erupting into uncontrolled violence. Now there is no such

156

outle.. If we want to avoid having Chandakha blow up in our faces, we'll have to disperse the population, reduce its density."

"But the other continents on the planet are uninhabitable."

Yvette now felt it was her turn to speak. "There are other planets, some very sparsely settled as yet, where the Chandakhari's knowledge of agriculture could be invaluable. I would suggest sponsoring a series of cash grants to encourage the citizens of Chandakha to move elsewhere. Many of them are desperate enough to accept such an offer."

"Ah yes," the Head smiled, "but now we run into a question of money—money to encourage them to leave Chandakha, money to transport them elsewhere, money to help the emigrés relocate on their new planet. Where, pray tell, is all this money going to come from?"

"Simple," Yvette explained. "Vesa has more than enough coming in; they scarcely know what to do with it all. And now that the murderers are out of the way, there'll be more money there than ever. The Emperor could authorize the Duke of Chandakha to levy a special tax for the purpose, to be paid by all the merchants of Vesa. In the long run it would be a small price for them to pay for security."

The Head's smile broadened immensely. "I really do like the way you two think—especially since your thoughts parallel my own so nicely. Just yesterday morning I sent the Emperor a note detailing a plan almost identical to the one you just suggested."

Jules looked startled. "You did?"

"Yes, occasionally this old man has an idea or two himself," laughed the Head with a twinkle in his eye. "After all, it's not enough for us to detect trouble after it's brewing. The Service is ultimately responsible for the total security of the Empire, and that includes finding the danger zones before they flare up; that way, remedying the problem is usually much simpler. I admit we failed the first time on Chandakha, which is why I'm doubly anxious to avoid repeating the mistake."

"Do you think the Emperor will follow your advice?" Yvette asked.

"Bill knows me pretty well by now, and he knows I don't make such recommendations lightly. I can almost guarantee he'll act as we suggest. He was already agreeing to my suggestion for the new Marchioness of Vesa."

"Yes, that was something I was wondering myself. What about Gindri?" Jules asked.

The Head sighed. "Gindri Lohlatt was a very weak woman, completely dominated by Garst. She knew what was going on, but had no inclination to stop it as long as she got everything she wanted. She'll be hauled up before a High Court of Justice, and condemnation by her peers is inevitable. I suspect they'll vote to banish her to Gastonia rather than have her executed—it's a sentence equivalent to death in any case, since her heart will never be able to stand the strain of an Earth-normal gravity like Gastonia's. In any event, that leaves the title open, since she has no heirs. I recommended to His Majesty that he appoint Marask Kantana as the new Marchioness of Vesa, and he agreed."

"Of course," Yvette smiled. "She's the perfect choice."

"Yes," said the Grand Duke of Sector Four, "I thought so, too. But she turned it down."

"What?" Jules and Yvette exclaimed, practically in unison.

"She thought she could be of more use to the Empire by continuing in SOTE—and I have to admit, I was sorry at the thought of losing her. Since she felt so strongly about the subject, the Emperor agreed to grant her request. He's now studying the various other political nominees who have come forward."

"Kantana's damned good," Jules commented. "I think it's a shame for her to get stuck on a backwater planet like Chandakha."

"So do I, so I dug out her records. Do you know she'd never been given the thousand-point test? She rose to her position as Chief entirely through the ranks, starting out as an ordinary field agent—and since Chandakha is such a comparatively minor world, nobody paid her any attention. I ordered the situation rectified immediately and discovered, not much to my surprise, that her score is nine ninety-six."

Jules gave out a low whistle. The thousand-point test was an examination of the total person, both physically and mentally. Currently Jules was the only thousand pointer alive, with his sister only a point below him. For Kantana to rank so highly was a considerable compliment.

"Yes indeed." The Head was amused by Jules' reaction. "As soon as her wrap-up on Vesa is complete, I'm having her reassigned as a special executive assistant to myself. She's going to be in charge of visiting as many planets as she can and spotting potential trouble zones like Chandakha before they ignite."

"I know she'll do an outstanding job," Yvette said. "She may even eliminate the need for *us* altogether."

Their boss shook his head. "There are some thirteen hundred planets in our Empire. Good as Kantana is, she can't be everywhere at once. No, my friends, as long as there is human greed and corruption, there will always be a need of your very special services."

And, as usual, he was right.